Who's
Tending the Store?

Janice Parris

Dedication

Special dedication to Jackie George Williams.

You left us too soon but, before you left, you made sure to take care of me like you always have. You sent Marva to help me type up my book. You were so proud that I was writing it and going to help Human Trafficking victims. You always said I was the front liner for the 49ers, and this would give me another reason to fight for the lives of others. I can hear you laughing now. Thank you for being an awesome big sister! You're forever in my heart and truly missed.

I want to dedicate this book to my son, Jahmaz Dawud Bealer, my best friend though he was from my womb. There wasn't a secret he kept from me, good or bad. The laughs we shared were hilarious even if they weren't right. He looked like his dad but had my humor, hair and feet. He was one of a kind. The friend that would just check up on you to make sure you were okay. I'm so glad God allowed me to spend time with my son. At 15, he was hit by a drunk driver and almost lost his life, and even could've been paralyzed. But God chose to let him live and, at 36, he became the father of an amazing little boy. Although Jahmaz isn't here anymore, he left us the gift of someone who reminds us of him, Mazz. I'm dedicating this to you, my love! I hope I made you proud.

Acknowledgements

To my Bishop John & Pastor Isha Edmondson, thank you for listening to the Holy Spirit when you spoke that we had books inside us. My spirit grabbed a hold and here I am today an author!

Carmen Scott, you were the first one to sit down with me and go over the layout of what it would take to get started. Thank you for the sleepovers and dedication.

Rondell Sherard, the long hours of discussing the book; you never got tired of hearing me talking about, helping it come alive and being engaged for months on it

Marva Jernigan, you came on board when Jackie asked you to help me type up my book and you did it with no hesitation. All the long Friday nights, Woodbury library runs, and our therapeutic talks helped get this done.

Shawn Suiter, you believed in me. All the tireless hours at the Woodbury Library helped get the book done, you typed your heart out. Your time spent meant the world to me.

Connie Barr, you stepped in when needed and your time was appreciated. Thank you for being part of the editing party!

Kenyetta Artis, you were my first editor. The sleepovers, early mornings, and late nights; and keeping me focused helped me get through each page.

April Holmes, you shared your author experience and put the book in order, you were the "cleanup" woman, showing me direction on how it needed to flow. You were the eyes in helping my vision of the book cover come to life and being there in the final hours.

Cousin Carolyn Holland, you answered every phone call; gave me your experience as a seven-time author from beginning to end. From editing to marketing & publishing, your encouragement gave me the confidence that I needed.

Karim Fletcher, you were patient with my many changes on the book cover. You captured my vision for Who's Tending the Store, and I appreciate you with your gift of design. KARIM FLETCHET K&S Custom Designs LLC

Giselle Ogando, to my amazing editor thank you for treating my book as if it was your own from start to finish. You gave me so much confidence in believing that my book would reach millions to help stop human trafficking.

Ten'ah Parris, my one and only daughter, I love you! Thank you for my two grandchildren, Jah'siy and Sky. You are just as amazed as I am with the release of my 1st book and your belief in me gave me the push that kept me going.

Chapter 1

A Day in the Life

Just an ordinary, 86-degree-day in Newark, New Jersey. At least, for those of us who grew up in the Brick City, it's what we'd pretty much call normal. Noisy streets, music blasting, pimped out rides, neighbors hanging outside; something was always moving. Screaming kids having fun as they run through the open fire hydrant, your usual neighborhood action. Jean was sitting in the window playing her favorite song by Marvin Gaye. Bett is planted on the stoop right below. Sheeka, Nia, and the girls are playing double-dutch out in front of "the Bricks", which is really a nickname for our huge brownstone with multiple apartments. Mr. Willie, as usual, sits in front of his cleaners, reading his newspaper and trying to be attentive of the heavy drug flow in the neighborhood. The twins, Ronnie and Ricky, are trapping for Ms. Kat on the corner. Everybody knows it but they will never say it out loud.

Adjacent to the Bricks is Tony's Bodega. Everyone in the neighborhood knew and loved Mr. Tony. This particular day, he was training his 24-year-old nephew Rico, who stays in trouble and went to live with Mr. Tony from Puerto Rico. He hoped Rico would turn his life around to ease his sister's worries since Rico is her only child, though he's anything but a child. Mr. Tony comes out and waves to the neighbors on the stoop and Mr. Willie waved back watching as he and Rico went back inside the store. He was teaching Rico the day-to-day operation of the store, going over the prices and truck deliveries. The twins checked Rico out because he's a new face. They are regulars at the bodega, but Mr. Tony isn't fond of them, so he always watches them closely because they sling drugs on the corner.

The twins entered the store and ordered a plate of Spanish food, stewed chicken, yellow rice and gandules with something to drink. Ricky nods at Rico, "What's up?"

Rico nods back, "What's up, man?"

"Are you new around here?"

"Yeah."

"We'll be outside, holla at us." The guys pay for their food and leave. Mr. Tony heard the conversation and told Rico not to mess with those boys because they are bad news. Rico couldn't help but to ask, "Bad news?"

"They sell drugs on the corner. A lot of people are strung out in this neighborhood."

"Do they make a lot of money?"

"I told you to stay away from them!"

Suddenly, Shae enters the store sharing a laugh with a man Mr. Tony had never seen before. "Hey Mr. Tony. I want you to meet my man, Larry." Larry says nonchalantly, "Wassup...." Mr. Tony smiles, "Hello, young man. Shae, how are you?"

"I'm doing well, I just got a raise and I want to get a house to move out of these bricks. I have been here for 18 years and I am ready to go. Larry's going to help me," as she points to him. "He works for the transportation department." Larry sarcastically interrupts, "You don't have to be telling him all of my damn business!" Rico looked up as Mr. Tony responds, "Easy Larry, Shae's a good friend of mine. I've been knowing her for years."

Larry gets agitated and tells Shae, "Get what you got to get and let's go." Shae looks at Mr. Tony and raises her eyebrows, pays for her stuff, and leaves. As soon as they walked out the door, Rico asked, "What's all that about?" Mr. Tony sighed as he answered, "Shae has had about twenty boyfriends over eighteen years since I met her, and they are always the "one". She has three kids with different fathers. I can say she's a hardworking mother. She's a beautiful person. Always looking for love but never finds it."

In walked Jean., "Hey Tony!" "Hey Jean," Mr. Tony replies, "how are you?"

Jean exhales, "Fine. Have you heard we're getting our building remodeled in a week? Supposedly, every apartment will be upgraded. We're going to stay in a hotel while my apartment is being done but we'll see if that happens!" They both laugh. As Jean walks out; Sheeka, Nia, and their two friends walk in to buy ice cream on this scorching hot day. Rico runs over anxiously to serve them.

"Hey ladies, how are you doing?" Rico anxiously strikes up a conversation with the girls, putting on his most charming smile. Sheeka answered, "I'm good. Who are you? I have never seen you before." Rico laughs, "I'm Rico, Mr. Tony's nephew."

"Where did you come from…Puerto Rico?" They all laughed.

Rico smiled, "Yeah."

Nia interjected, "It's pretty over there. I've seen pictures. Why did you leave that beautiful place to come here?" Rico let out a deep sigh before answering, "I got into some trouble," then quickly changed the subject. "What would you like to buy?" Nia answered, "I want a lemon ICEE." Rico replied, "Oh...so you like lemon?" "Yeah, it's my favorite." Sheeka and the other girls ordered cherry, Rico served the girls still wearing a flirtatious smile on his face. They paid him and waved, "See you tomorrow!" Rico nods an okay and watched them walk out the door.

As the young girls crossed the street, they heard arguing from the open window in Shae's apartment. They hear screaming, "Leave me alone! You always think someone wants me. You're so dumb!" Suddenly, they heard a loud smack and a faint scream. Everyone stopped what they were doing and looked up at the window. A minute passes and there's dead silence, so everyone goes on about their business. Mr. Willie is waiting on Rev. Briggs who was getting his dry cleaning. Rev. Briggs mentioned that he heard the commotion. Mr. Willie shook his head, "That girl is going to get hurt one day. She's always bringing in one guy after another. You're bound to get your hand caught in a trap eventually." Rev. Briggs agreed, "I'll have a talk with her. She always has an open ear. God has protected her this far. You have to keep on praying for her."

A few minutes later, Larry exits the building popping his collar and throwing on his shades, looking a little upset. He walked down the steps and bumped into Kat as he passed in a hurry.

Kat yells, "Yo!, you got a problem?!" Larry looked back at her, "What?!" As he turns around quickly, "You're gonna have a problem if you don't get the hell out my face!" Kat grits her teeth and leans forward, "You got the wrong one. I ain't Shae!" Larry laughed her reply off and walked back to his car, a four door, Candy Apple Red 1964 Ford Galaxy. He never looks back as he drives off with his top down and shades on. Jean called Kat over and asked, "Are you good?" Kat, still fuming, answered her, "I'm good, but he might not be." Then Kat yelled, "Yo Ricky, you're supposed to be looking out. You didn't see that?"

"Oh I saw it alright. I got this!" Then Jean asked, "Did you hear all that hollering coming from Shae's apartment?" Kat replied, "Yeah, but you know that's been going on for years." Then she continued, "If she likes it, I love it."

Just then Monster, Shae's son, walked up the steps and into the apartment, "Oh My God!!" A scream came from the window. Then he ran to Jean's apartment; banging on her door, still screaming, "Ms. Jean call 911!!! My mom is unconscious!"

He ran back to the apartment and tried to wake her up. Jean called the police. Ronnie and Ricky heard Monster's cries for his mom and started running up the steps. Ricky asked, "Monster, where does her boyfriend live? He's the one who left out of here!" Monster was furious. Kat came up to the apartment and sent Ronnie and Ricky out because the cops and ambulance were approaching.

When the police arrive, Kat and Jean wouldn't give up any information to the police. Bett had walked to the pharmacy and ran back down the street as she saw flashing lights by the building, not knowing what's going on. See, in the Bricks, everyone is like family ever since she was little. Bett probed frantically, "What happened? What happened?" The police had to hold her back. But she persisted, "What's going on, is someone sick?" Out comes Boots from the alley and gets right near Bett, "It's your momma. The twenty-sixth boyfriend beat the daylights out of her…well, no, it's about 6 pm, so he beat the night lights out of her. Hell, he beat her ass!" Bypassing his comments, Bett cried, "Officer, officer! It's my mom. Is she okay?" The officer said, "Miss, they are trying to stabilize her now. She'll be heading to University Hospital and you can see her then."

As she's talking to the officer, Monster ran out towards Mr. Tony's store and Rico was watching

12

from the corner. Monster was pissed and pacing back and forth. Bett tried to calm him down enough to find out what happened when Rico asks Monster, "Yo dude, you alright man? What happened over there?"

"That Bastard hit my mother! That sorry, no good…." Rico cut him off before he could finish talking. "Who is your mother?"

"Shae is my mother! Who the hell are you anyhow?"

"Was it your mom's fiancé, Larry?"

"Fiancé! I'll kill somebody over my mother!" He screamed, "Ahhhhhhhhhhh!"

"Chill, man. Where can I find him?"

"Who Larry? He's probably at the pool hall on 3rd."

"At the pool hall?"

"Yeah, why?"

"I thought you might wanna go check him out."

Monster replied after thinking things through, "Nah…he's not worth it, but I'll kill for my mother. She's all I have." Rico replied, "Yo, you got a level head. Whose been schooling you, young boy?" Monster tells him, "Rev. Briggs. He's my mentor."

"Looks like he's got in your head." Monster lets out a sigh, "Maybe so."

Rev Briggs rushes over to Monster, "Son, is your mom okay?" Monster answered, "I'm not sure sir, her face looked really bad. It was all swollen and her lip was busted." Rev. Briggs reassuringly tells him, "Everything is going to be okay." But Monster never answered. "You're not losing your faith are you son?" Rev. Briggs asked. "In times like this, you need to fight the devil. Fight! You hear me!"

Hearing their conversation, Rico laughed to himself.... "What devil? He needs to fight Larry. No, he needs to whip his ass!"

Rev. Briggs turned to Rico, "Violence doesn't fix things, prayer does!" Then, Rico got called in by his uncle. Rico yelled back, "Okay, tio." Then turned to Rev. Briggs saying, "They'd be praying for Larry, if it was my mother."

"Rico, where were you? Why do you keep disappearing? You don't even know anybody here. Stay focused boy, stay focused! Your life is here, not in the streets!" Mr. Tony says to Rico and starts yelling in Spanish, "Vamos, it's almost closing time. Para la casa." So he goes to check the surveillance tapes for the day because of the frequent drug activity behind the store. When he went in the back room to review the tapes and he sees Rico talking to Quianna, a seventeen year-old girl from the neighborhood. She hugged him and gave up her phone number. Mr. Tony looked surprised, saying to himself, 'So that's where he was, boy work fast!'

The ambulance didn't take long to leave with Shae as she went in and out of consciousness. Once Jean saw Shae's face, she said to herself, 'If the police ask again, I'll tell them what I witnessed.' This was the worst beating they saw Shae get.

It was 7:00 pm and the members of the church choir gathered for choir rehearsal. Before rehearsal started, they said a prayer for Shae. 'Father, we thank you for this day. We are praying for healing and wholeness over Shae in the name of Jesus. God touch her life and make her complete. Fill the void that you know only you can fill, make her rugged places straight and anoint the hands that touch her. In Jesus' name.' "Everyone please keep Shae and her family in prayer," the director announced as soon as they finished. Once the singing began, you could hear it from the street.

Rev. Briggs stood outside the church, talking to Mr. Willie as he closed the gate to the cleaners which stayed open an hour later than usual because of the commotion. In conversation, he asked Mr. Willie, "Have you met Tony's nephew?"

"I've seen him talking to the boys on the corner. Those are not the first people you want to meet. Why did you ask Briggs?" Mr. Willie countered.

"I just asked."

"No Briggs, what is it?"

Rev. Briggs answered, "I was just trying to calm Monster down. You know I've had him under my wing for some time and he's doing well. That young man was trying to get Monster fired up about his mother. He didn't react, while I was there. You know the enemy will try to rear his ugly head, but God is able to keep him from falling. Pray for Monster, Willie."

"I will and, if I see him with those boys, I'll call him to help me at the Cleaners."

"Thanks, man. I'm leaving, I'll see you tomorrow."

Mr. Willie nods, "Okay, Briggs."

Not too long after, the police pulled off and all the action was over. But the street was still buzzing. Kat sat on the stoop with Ronnie and Ricky. Mr. Tony closed his bodega for the night, so Rico walked over to the stoop. "What's up?" Rico uttered striking up conversation, "Everything alright over here?" No one answered. Kat continued talking to Ronnie and Ricky, scolding them for not doing more with Larry. "I want something done and I mean it. He lives on Peach Street but he's always at the pool hall. Find him and I got you."

Rico interrupted again, "Does that include me too?" But no one said anything, and everybody went their separate ways. Kat went in the house and the boys returned to their corner. Not willing to give up, Rico followed them and engages in a conversation.

Chapter 2

Weekend at the 'Bricks'

Quianna walked by the boys and says, "What's up Rico?" Rico smiled and winked, "What's up," as he checked her out from her legs, making his way up with a deviant smile on his face. Ricky caught a weird vibe and asked Rico, "What you know about Key?"

"I don't, why…is she your girl?" Ricky smirked, "Something like that…that's my shorty." And they both laughed.

Rico started heading up to Main Street. He passed by 2 stores and walked 3 more blocks before seeing the pool hall. He goes in and, through the clouds of cigarette smoke, sees Larry standing by a pool table. Larry didn't remember him from the store, so they played a game of pool. Rico has some good shots and cleaned up the table, so Larry is intrigued and pursues a conversation with Rico.

Larry tells Rico that he works for the Transportation Department. Rico stated, "Oh yeah? I'm new here and need a job."

"I can get someone to get you an interview."

Rico nods his head, "That would be cool!"

"Okay, tomorrow then?"

"Yeah. Where do you want to meet?"

"Right here at 7:00 pm." Rico agrees, "Alright, later man." They shake on it and Rico left the hall.

Boots was walking home, back to the alley, when he sees the two little middle school girls that were playing with Sheeka and Nia talking to Rico. Not sure of what's going on, Boots watches from the alley and sees Rico give them money, then walk off. Wondering what that was all about, Boots kept walking.

It's Friday night, so as usual, Quianna gets dropped off home by her karate teacher, Chan. Her mom, Tootie, came home afterwards. When she sees Tootie pull up, Jean comes down giving her the low-down of today's activities as she opens her mail. While she's half-listening to Jean, Tootie finds out that her apartment is getting remodeled first and has one week to get her personal belongings together. Shae's apartment will be done at the same time. Tootie turns her attention back to Jean and asks if Shae is okay and if she should go to the hospital. But Jean told her no and adds, "Her children are up there, but I didn't see Blue." Blue is Shae's oldest boy.

It's right around 9:00 pm and getting dark, Choir rehearsal is over. One lady who is a choir member walked over to the stoop to tell Jean and Tootie that she's praying for Shae and asked if they had heard anything further from the hospital. They both answered no. Then, Tootie blurts out, "I'm going to the hospital to check on her. That's my friend, we've been on the top floor for years." She tells Quianna to go in and do her homework and get something to eat. Tootie lets Jean know that she will give her an update when she gets there. Despite what her mom says, Quianna never goes in the house. A few minutes after Tootie left, Ricky comes over to sit on the stoop and asks, "What's up Key, What's up with you? Looking good ma...."

But their conversation gets interrupted by this car turning the corner real slow and looking suspicious. It was candy apple red, dark tints on all the windows, headlights off. Ricky goes in his waist band and tells Key to go in the house, but she runs through the alley instead, passing Boots and running into Rico, as she gasped for air.

"Why are you running?" Rico asked as he held both her arms.

"I think there may be a shootout, I'm scared...this old red car and Ricky...." Then Rico motions for her to come closer, and he hugs her and pulls her close to protect her. "I got you, don't be afraid." He kisses her cheek and then moves to her lips. Boots was watching and kicks a can in disruption. Quianna realized that he was still there so she pulls away from Rico and tells him, "I have to go." She heads down the alley towards Boots. Quianna asked Boots if he heard any shots. "I think that was Ms. Shae's boyfriend in that car." Boots replied, "There's going to be shots in your ass, messing with that boy. He's too old for you. You're a smart girl doing dumb stuff. Make up your mind...are you smart or dumb?"

"You always check me Mr. Boots. Always! I think you are the only one who cares about me. So, let me ask you a question - how did you end up like this?"

"What - in the alley?"

"Yeah." Boots takes a deep breath. "I was a stockbroker on Wall Street in New York and did drugs with some colleagues of mine and then that wasn't enough. I had a wife and a daughter, but the lifestyle I was living was not conducive to that of a family man. Things got bigger and went faster than I was ready for and here I am." Boots shrugged as he changed the subject, "Let me see what's going on around front before you try to go in." After making sure it was safe for her to go in, he calls for her to come. He tells her good night, and she smiles, "Good night." She gives him a hug, "I love you too Mr. Boots," with playful sarcasm in her tone, she goes in the house.

Meanwhile, Tootie arrives at University Hospital to check on Shae. Shae had a broken eye socket and nose, but Tootie was told she'd be okay. Tootie asked Bett, who was sitting in the waiting room, where Blue was. Bett responded, "He broke his phone a few days ago and we haven't heard from him. He works at Chelsey's Gentlemen's Club, he's the manager."

"What time does he get off? Do you want me to tell him about your mom?"

"Naaah, he has a temper. I think it's best that we tell him when he gets home."

"So you're saying if your mom is all beat up and busted that you wouldn't want your family to let you know?"

"I just don't want him to get himself in any trouble - he don't play. He's just like, his dad Chauncey." Tootie laughed, "Oh yeah the dresser."

Bett replied sarcastically, "Yea, him. If he heard about this, he'd track Larry down and beat the shit out of him." Tootie decided to leave, "Okay, I'm heading out, just wanted to check on my friend."

"Okay Ms. Tootie, thank you so much."

"No problem baby, we're family."

Still, all the way home it bothered Tootie that Blue didn't know, so she headed to Chelsey's. As she approached the place and began to park, she grabs for her phone when this candy apple red car rolls around slowly. She realized it was Larry's car. Tootie thought if she went into the club, she could go in and call the police, but that would mess up everyone's good time. So she waited for Larry to go in first and then she'd go in to tell Blue about his mom. Five minutes pass, Tootie gets out and heads into the establishment. She was looking around hesitantly because it was dimly lit and close to the woods. She opens the door and sees the bouncer. Approaching him, she asks, "I need to talk to Blue, is he around?" The bouncer glanced at her nurse scrubs and the crocs on her feet for a minute, then asks for her name. "Wait here a minute, I'll call him." Three minutes pass by and then Blue comes to the door.

"Hey, Ms. Tootie. What are you doing here?" Tootie tries to stay calm while telling him, "There was an accident. It's your mother." Blue wasn't sure he heard her right, "My mother?" Tootie continues, "Yes, she was beaten severely."

Confused, he asks, "Was she robbed?"

"No, her boyfriend beat her up."

"Wait, what? Her boyfriend?!" Tootie clarifies for him, "You know Larry with the candy apple red car?" "No, I've only seen him once. I'm usually at my girl's or at the club. How do I find this joker?"

"Now Blue, what exactly are you planning to do? I don't want you getting into any trouble!"

"I can't promise you anything. Wait…how is she?" He begins to get filled with rage as he clenches his fists. Tootie tries to calm him down, but Blue kept pressing, "What's his name again?"

"His name is Larry. He fractured her eye socket, and she has a broken nose, but the doctor says she'll be fine."

"Where can I find him Ms. Tootie? Please…now, you came this far, help me find this dude!" Tootie looks at him, hearing the pain in his voice and says, "Okay Blue." She places her hands on his chest and tells him, "You won't have to look far because I saw him come in here right before I got here."

"He's still here? What does he have on?" Tootie pleads with him, "Blue, please give me time to get to my car." Blue assures her and says, "Sure Ms. Tootie." "He has on a pink collared shirt, white tee and black cargo pants." Then she turned around to leave.

Two minutes passed and Tootie was safely in her car, but she waited to see what would happen. Ten minutes later people start running from the club. Strippers running out half naked, screams coming from all directions. The club looked like it was almost cleared out but there was no sign of Blue and Larry. They must still be fighting, that or someone is hurt by now. Finally, Blue emerges without Larry. He looked like something had happened, but it didn't look like a fight took place.

Tootie kept watching as Blue paced back and forth in the parking lot. All of a sudden, the door flies open and Larry rushes Blue with all his might, but Blue quickly moves out of the way and Larry falls flat on his face. Blue jumps on his back and starts beating him. He's hitting Larry with blows on both sides of his head. The club patrons and workers let this go on for about 20 seconds, then the bouncers pull Blue off him. Larry laid motionless on the blacktop. Blue broke away from the guys and goes back over to Larry and kicks him in his head. One of the bouncers tells him, "Alright man, that's enough." Blue stormed back inside the club, grabbed his book bag and left. Larry was still lying face down bleeding and nobody was trying to help him. One of the bouncers walked over to check if he was breathing. He was, so they picked him up and threw him in his convertible and went back inside. The club was shut down for the night.

Back at the Bricks, Rico called Quianna, "Hey girl, what are you doing?" "I just took a shower and I'm about to take it down."

"Oh, really? I'd like to have been in that shower with you."

"Whatever Rico, what's up? I have to get some sleep, I have finals next week and I have to...." Quianna pauses, "I hear my mom, gotta go...bye!" Tootie peeped into her room to see if she's still awake. "Hey pumpkin." Quianna greets her back, "Hey mom, how's Ms. Shae?"

"She's pretty beaten up, but she'll be fine." They hear a door slam across the hall. Tootie goes out into the hallway to see who it is but no one was there. She knocks on Shae's door and Blue opens it. She asks him, "Are you okay?" Blue answered, "I'm fine. My mom's house doesn't look too messed up." Tootie asked, "So what happened at the club?" He tells her, "I beat his ass. I don't think he'll be coming around here anymore. I'm about to change my clothes and go check on my mom." Tootie mentioned, "It's after visiting hours but tell them it's your mom and they'll let you see her."

Chapter 3

Sunday Morning Vibes

Everyone at the Bricks starts their day pretty early on Sunday's, especially in the summer. Mr. Willie opens his door and comes outside to sit on the old wooden bench in front of his store. The church members are arriving for Sunday service. Rev. Briggs arrives and greets Mr. Willie as usual. Rev. Briggs asks him, "Are you coming to church today, Deacon Willie?" "Yes, I'll be there late as usual," he answered.

Rev. Briggs retorts, "Is God late when you need him?"

"No, never."

"My point exactly, Deacon Willie!"

The Praise and Worship Team starts, and you can hear them all the way down the block. The anointing is thick! Bett comes out and sits as usual on the stoop and Blue joins her. Jean is in the window with a cup of coffee. Rex pulls up in front of the building. He gets out and greets her, "Hey Jean."

"Hey, Rex."

Rex was fairly new to the neighborhood and had moved up from Louisiana a couple of years ago. But he had fallen for Jean the moment he met her.

"Are you coming to service?" Rex asked.

"No, I'm going to sit right here by this window, drink my coffee, and praise the Lord while folding these clothes. The music does sound good."

"I sure would have liked if you had joined me. Can I come over when I get out?"

"We'll see, Rex."

"I'm not going to wait for benediction. I'm running out the church so I can see my baby!"

Jean laughed, "See, there you go. You better stay and wait on Jesus!" Rex chuckles back and says, "The music is powerful."

Bett looks over at Blue as if extending an invitation, "I'm going over to the church." Blue, staring at the parked cars on the street, says "I'm coming with you, we need to pray for mom, things have gone too far." Just then, Monster comes out dressed for church as he sees Bett and Blue getting up. Taken off guard, Monster asked, "Where are you going?" Blue answered, "To church with your ugly butt!" Monster thought they were joking, "No, seriously. Where are you going?" Now Bett answered, "To church for real man!" Monster looked up to heaven and put his hands together, "Thank you Jesus for answering my prayers!" Suddenly, Blue puts him in a headlock, and they all walked over to the church. The anointing was flowing, and you could feel it even before getting to the door. Ms. Tootie walked over in her dark purple dress with buttons down the back and her cream-colored heels. Ms. Kat sat on the steps, deafened by the sound of the drums, guitars, and the piano. The church doors were wide open, and you can see right up to the pulpit.

Rev. Briggs begins his service, "What's holding you back? Sometimes people make excuses for many different things, like I don't have the right education or I'm not smart enough. I never finished school, or I wasn't trained on that yet. Nobody taught me, or simply, I'm scared - what if I'm not good enough, I might fail! Well, the enemy wants you to think that you can't make it. That you're inadequate. But God says the opposite. He says, 'I can do all things through Christ that strengthens me. I am more than a conqueror.' To strengthen means to reinforce, to toughen, to redouble, make stronger or to beef up. To conquer means to overcome, overpower, overthrow, to get the better of, to rise above, or to beat. So, I ask again, what is holding you back? If God has equipped you with strength, then you can push through the obstacle course of life. If he has equipped you with conquering, then you already know, you have the ability to win. If you are victorious, which you are, then the thing you're going through isn't over until you win!"

After Rev, Briggs got done preaching, it was time for the call to salvation and 18 people were saved. Bett and Blue stood up at the same time and walked to the altar. Monster, with tears flowing down his face, praised God for answering his prayers for his family.

He prayed, "God save my mom, make her whole and complete in You, Heavenly Father." Now it was time for the benediction.

Monster leaves out and crosses the street when Quianna and Jean's daughter, Te'nah, stop to talk to him. Te'nah starts by saying, "That was a good service. I want to get my life right, I mean it. I'm not happy with the way I'm living." Tears start welling up in her eyes. Monster assures her, "God is able to change you Nae, just give Him a chance." He holds her as she cries on his shoulder. Quianna rubs her back fighting off the tears in her own eyes. Boots had made his way to the stoop, where Bett and Blue had already taken back their spots, and adds, "That was a good service! I was about to come over there!" Bett smirked, "Yea right!" Boots replied, "I go over there every now and then, but I listen every Sunday." Ronnie, who had been sitting on the stoop throughout the whole service, interjected, "They had me crying, I was trying to be hard, but...forget it;" he tries to get himself together.

After service, Jean and Rex were in his car headed to lunch as they passed 2 of the four girls who were talking to Rico in the back of the alley. Jean and Rex turn the corner, and the sight of Rico and the girls disturbed her.

"Rex why is that grown ass man talking to them babies?" Rex replied, "Jean don't you know him?"

"Yeah, sort of, that's Tony's nephew."

"Okay, maybe he knows the girls from the store, stop thinking the worst!"

Rico, absorbed in his conversation with the girls, asked them, "What are you all up to?" Sheeka responds, "Nothing just sitting on the stoop." "Are you even allowed off the block?"

Nia replied, "I am but have to be back by seven." Sheeka says, "I can, but I have to tell my mom where I'm going. Why?"

Rico explained, "Cause there's going to be a carnival coming on Friday and I was going to treat you all, but you can't tell anyone cause I'm new around here. Your parents probably won't let you go." Nia promised she wouldn't say anything. Sheeka boasted with excitement, "I can tell my mom I'm going over Nikki's house!" "Me too!" Nia jumped in. Rico tells the girls to promise they won't say anything, or they can't go. The girl's eyes gleam with excitement as they pinky promise not to say anything to anyone.

Rico left the girls heading to the pool hall and talking on his phone. When he reaches the pool hall, he asked some of the patrons, "Where's Larry?" The patrons responded that they hadn't seen Larry since last night. Rico decided to play several games of pool while he waited. Then, he took a break, and a call came in. He answered it and tells the caller, "The dude Larry's not here. I'll call an Uber to come get ya'll." His cousin and some friends had just arrived from Puerto Rico and were waiting to get picked up at the Newark International Airport.

Meanwhile, Tootie was leaving out for work and took a detour past the gentlemen's club where she saw Larry's car still parked in the same spot. Tootie pulled over. She carefully closes her door and slowly walks up to Larry's car. After looking into the car she realizes he isn't in there, so she goes back to her car. Suddenly, she hears someone say, "Are you looking for the man who was in that car?" Tootie responds quickly, "Yes, do you know where he is?" "He went walking down the street early this morning." Tootie shouted out "Okay, thank you!" as she jumps back in her car. She left not knowing what to think. Her mind was racing. 'Is he hurt or not? Why did he leave hours after the incident?'

In the meantime, Larry had gone to his cousin's house, who only lived a couple of blocks away, to recover. He was upset and wanted revenge. His cousin Mook and 2 of his boys went looking for Blue. As they left the house, Tootie spotted Larry climb in the back of the black Chrysler. She ducked her head and decided to follow them. They first go past the Bricks and pass the corner. Ronnie and Ricky look to see who's in the car, but they didn't see Larry. Next, they headed to Blue's girl's house. Tootie continued to follow them. When she saw them slowing down, she parked her car near the corner. The guys roll past the girlfriend's house with no sign of Blue or his car, so they leave. But not before they notice the girlfriend's cousin leaving the corner store. Mook stopped the car, they jumped out and beat him with a bat, "Tell

Blue, he's next!" The boy laid helpless on the sidewalk and they got back in the car and left.

Tootie was frightened at what she had just seen so she heads back to the apartment and calls out of work. She asked everyone if they knew how to get in touch with Blue. She found Jean and told her what had happened. Jean called Blue and warned him not to go to his girlfriend's house and to watch his back. She told him Larry's boys were looking for him. Tootie went in the house and watched out the back window near the fire escape, feeling terrified, replaying the scene from the corner store in her mind. Jean told Kat what was going on and Kat went to Ricky and Ronnie warning them to keep their eyes opened. The twins called the boys from around the way, and they all sat by the steps waiting.

While all this was going down, Rico's people were in the streets checking out the neighborhood, up to no good. They were five deep, in a dark blue minivan with black tints on the back windows. They passed by Mr. Tony's store and then by the 'Bricks'. Rico sat in the back where he couldn't be seen. They headed back to the hotel near the airport where they requested adjoining rooms with two double beds on the ground floor. The crew headed to Albany, NY after check-out on Monday.

Chapter 4

Skipping School

It's Monday morning; and Sheeka and Nia head out for school as usual. The end of school year was near, and they're excited about going to middle school next year. On their way to school, Sheeka gets a call from Rico.

"Hey Sheeka, what's up? What are you doing?"

She replies, "On my way to school."

"You and Nia want to hang out with me and my boys?"

"I guess...hangout where?"

"The beach, Coney Island."

Sheeka responds, hesitation resounding in her tone, "When?" Rico, not wanting to sound too excited, stated calmly, "Now if you want."

Her voice starts to quiver now as she continues, "Uhm, let me ask Nia. I'm not too sure about this Rico." Rico puts on his charming voice and says, "Come on...it will be fun. My boys and I will pay for everything. We'll have you home before school is over or at least by five. Will five o'clock be too late?" Sheeka reluctantly replies, "Five o'clock will be good. I will call you back." Rico senses the resistance in her voice. He tells her to call Nia while he is on the phone concerned she might not call him back. He lets out a chuckle to ease her. She agrees, never revealing that Nia was already with her, and mutes the phone. "Nia, Rico wants to know if you want to go hang out at Coney Island with him and his boys." Nia asked, "When?" Sheeka tells her that he wanted to hang out now and that he promised to have them back no later than five o'clock. Nia, reluctance in her voice, said; "I don't know, the school is going to call our parents." But Sheeka tells her that they can just say they were at school but came in late and that's why they were marked absent. "Come on Nia! We get to hang out with some older guys, and we will be the shit," Sheeka insisted.

But Nia was not feeling this at all, "I'm good, you go ahead if you want. I have a bad feeling we're going to get in trouble."

Sheeka unmutes her phone, "Hey Rico."

"Yeah?"

"We're gonna pass. Nia doesn't want to go."

Rico was a little frustrated and wanted to know why Nia didn't want to go. Sheeka said, "I don't know, she said the school is going to call our parents." Rico tried to further persuade her and says, "Okay, tell Nia not only will we pay for everything, but we'll give ya'll both fifty dollars a piece. Some extra spending money for you! We'll get you back before five, I promise." Sheeka puts him on hold and mutes the phone again. She repeats to Nia what Rico said and adds, "Look school is almost over for the year. Let's have some fun, fifty dollars Nia! Come on!" Nia hesitantly agrees, every fiber in her was against it, but she could see her best friend really liked Rico. Sheeka drops the phone with excitement. She picked it up, unmutes the phone and says, "Yes we're going!" Rico asked her if they drink and she answered hesitantly, "Yes, I guess. What do you have?" Rico tells her it's a surprise. She mentioned that they didn't have bathing suits, but he assured her that it would be okay because they needed swim trunks. So, she tells him to just pick her and Nia up and they can all go out together to get what they needed. Rico asked for their location, and she answered, "Halsey & Pearl."

Rico said he'd be there in twenty minutes in a dark blue minivan.

While waiting on the corner, Ms. Tootie pulled up. "Hey girls come on, I'll give you a ride to school."

"We're alright, Ms. Tootie. We'll walk." Sheeka and Nia looked at each other, hoping Ms. Tootie would drive off.

But Ms. Tootie wouldn't let up and says, "Girl get in this car. I'm already pulled over and I'm taking Quianna to school." Seeing no way out of this, they get in the car. Sheeka text Rico to let him know Quianna's mom had just picked them up. *'Change of plans. Miss Tootie is with us. Meet us at the middle school by Washington Place.'*

He texts her back, *'You have Quianna with you? Ask her if she wants to go too.'* Sheeka texts back, *'No, you ask her.'* Rico typed, *'okay.'* He texted Quianna and gives her the same spiel as the other two, and she goes for it.

Tootie drops them off at the adjacent schools. She yells out to the girls, "Have a great day!" The girls say their goodbyes as they exit the car.

Te'nah had also just arrived by public transportation and started walking to the school when she sees Sheeka, Quianna and Nia talking on the sidewalk. She briefly converses with them when the blue minivan pulls up with four men in it. Rico is in the passenger side now. They are all Spanish nice-looking muscular men. Te'nah starts walking away and Nia looks back at Te'nah with a reluctant stare as if she didn't want to be there. She didn't want to be there, and now having seen Rico's friends, she wanted to go even less. She almost looked as if she was being forced to go. Te'nah kept walking but couldn't get Nia's face out of her mind. She was also wondering why they would be going with the new guy at the store. They barely knew him.

It's third period, and Te'nah still can't shake her thoughts of Nia. She takes a moment to call Quianna just to ask her where they were going, but it goes straight to voicemail. She left a message asking only for a call back, assuming maybe they made it to class, and she had her phone turned off.

Over at University Hospital, Shae is being seen by the doctor and will be released today. She was scared, sitting on the bed all alone. Even though she had been beaten up, she still thought about Larry wondering if he still loved her. In her warped sense of love, she wanted to see him. She was hoping that he hadn't moved on to someone else. She thought, 'If she could get out of this hospital, they could work things out and she could profess her love to him.'

Mr. Willie was her first visitor of the day. Hopefully, within an hour or two she will be discharged. Mr. Willie asked Shae, "Are you okay?" "Yes Mr. Willie, thanks for coming to see me." She said she was fine, but Shae had a black eye which is swollen shut and a broken nose. She looked pretty bad, so Mr. Willie proceeds to tell Shae, "Look Shae, I've known you way too long. First, this has gone on way too long. Second, I love you like my own. Why do you keep going through this over again? Do you know your worth? You can't keep putting yourself in these relationships, putting yourself through this pain, and your kids. Your life is too valuable, Shae." Unsure of how to respond, Shae just stared at the dull beige wall of her room.

It was mid-afternoon, Rico and the girls were riding in the minivan, music is blasting, and the girls are jamming in the back with tinted windows. The guys tell them their next stop is for bathing suits. They got breakfast and passed it back to the girls. While the girls are eating breakfast, the guys take their opportunity and pass them tainted orange juice. They were all enjoying the music, eating, and drinking having a good time. Not too long after they had finished eating, Nia says her stomach feels funny and she becomes sleepy. Sheeka got worried and tried to tend to her but she became more and more disoriented with every move. She started feeling strange and passed out next. Quianna is witnessing all of this and becomes concerned. She yells out, "What the hell is going on?" She tries to fight it, but the stealth drug overpowered her. Soon, all three girls were knocked out in the back of the van. The guys merge onto the Garden State Parkway to Interstate 87 heading towards Albany. They pull up to an old blue two-story house with boarded up windows located a few minutes off the highway. Once they reached their destination the garage door opened, and they pulled the van inside the garage. They carried the girls inside the house and tied them to some chairs that were chained and bolted to the floor.

They taped their mouths, took off their clothes, and raped them while they were unconscious. The first one to wake up was Nia hours later. It was blurry, and she felt restrained and disoriented. She felt a painful sting from the waist down, something was different, something didn't feel right. Then, it was Quianna whose mouth was duct taped shut. Her whole body ached, but she was frantic because she is the oldest of the bunch. Though she was disheveled, she felt she had to protect the others since they were younger than her, they were only in middle school! They were all tied up together. Sheeka was still knocked out and hadn't come to consciousness yet. Tears filled Nia and Quianna's eyes at the realization of their surroundings.

The School Scene

During home room at the high school, Quianna was marked absent which isn't normal for her. She hadn't missed school all year. School was almost out, and she was a shoo-in for the perfect attendance award. The attendance monitor was alerted and called Tootie to ask if Quianna was sick. Tootie answered the phone, surprised by the gentleman's question, and replied, "No, I dropped her off at school this morning. I'm sorry but can you check again?" The monitor checked her classroom and sent a request over the intercom. He immediately let Ms. Tootie know that Quianna was nowhere on school property.

Tootie, now frightened more than upset started to cry. This isn't like Quianna. Her co-workers asked if she was okay, noticing her change in demeanor. She tried to gather herself, but she couldn't work any longer. Her mind was racing. Tootie tried to call Quianna, but it went straight to voicemail. She then called three more times. Still nothing. She left a message each time, growing more and more concerned with each call. She called Sheeka's mom, Vivian and asked her to try to reach Sheeka because they were together when she dropped them off. But Sheeka's mom said that nobody from the school contacted her and that Sheeka was in school. Vivian hung the phone up. After hanging up, Vivian says to herself, "Her fast ass daughter probably skipped school with one of the boys she always talking to." Tootie called Nia's mom, Renee, next. Renee told Tootie that Nia was also in school. She hadn't received a phone call all day. Just as Tootie was about to tell Renee about the school's phone call, Renee gets a call on the other line. It's the school.

Renee asked Tootie to hold on while she answered. The school monitor at Nia's school called to notify Renee that Nia was absent. Renee told her that Nia had left for school in the morning and she was not sure where she could be. Renee becomes worried because this is not Nia's character at all. Renee clicked back over to Tootie and told her the news of Nia's absence. Tootie replied, "Renee, I dropped Quianna, Sheeka and Nia off together. I hope they haven't played hooky." Renee asked, "So Vivian hasn't gotten a call about Sheeka? I'm going to three-way Vivian, hold on." The ladies connect the call to Vivian and ask if she heard anything. Vivian insists that she hadn't gotten a call, and proceeds to say, "I just don't think my daughter would do something like that." Renee and Tootie both say together, "Call the school!!" They hung up with Vivian, and she called the middle school to discover that Sheeka wasn't there either! Vivian called Renee back instantly and tells her that Sheeka isn't there. Vivian asked Renee, "What in the world is going on?" Renee told Vivian to hold on as she was going to call Tootie. Tootie answered right away and Renee merged the calls.

They tell Tootie that none of the girls are in school. Tootie tried to remember back to when she dropped them off. She remembers passing Te'nah. She wasn't sure if Te'nah had seen the girls, but she remembered seeing Te'nah get off the bus and heading in their direction. Tootie let the other ladies know that she was going to make some phone calls and would get back to them. She instructed them to get back to her if they heard anything. Vivian inquired, before they hang up, if any of the girls had boyfriends. She recalled playing hookie from school when she had a boyfriend. In a sense, she had hoped this was the case. Tootie replied, "I don't think so," and Renee answered with an attitude, "No, Nia don't have no boyfriend." The phone conversation went silent. After a couple of minutes, Tootie, finally, broke the silence with, "I don't know about ya'll but I'm going to beat Quianna's ass when she gets in here." Renee followed up, "Me too! I'm surprised at Nia. This isn't like her. I've never known her to be a follower." Vivian interrupted, "A follower? So, what are you trying to say, that our kids put your angel up to something?" Renee replied, "No,

I didn't say that. I'm just saying she's a little naive, but a smart girl." Tootie chimed in, "I don't know Renee I have to agree with Vivian. It sounds like you think your child is better than ours." Renee snapped back, "No I don't. I just know my child. Think what you want but don't put words in my mouth." Upset and now divided, they all hung up.

Chapter 5

The Missing Girls

Tootie called Quianna's phone again and it went to voicemail, same for Nia and Sheeka. Vivian jumped in her car to check out the parks. Tootie continues to make phone calls. She called her friends to see if anyone had seen her, to no avail. Five o'clock, evening time comes and still no sign of the girls. Their phones are still off. Vivian is worried now, she and Renee are out on the stoop. The word is getting around, as it typically travels quick at the "Bricks". Had anyone seen these girls? Te'nah walks up and Renee asks her, "Have you seen the girls, Nae?" Ten'ah shook her head yes, and says she saw them at the school. With slim hope, Renee asked her if she recalled the time. Te'nah said she wasn't sure of the time but that they were standing on the sidewalk talking to each other. Renee proceeded to ask if she had seen Quianna in class. But she had not. Renee, continuing her interrogation, asked if she knew who the girls would have hung out with. At that point, Te'nah lowered her head and replied solemnly, "No" as she walked away. Renee thought Te'nah was sad because of the girls' disappearance, but it was the guilt of knowing the truth.

Seven o'clock at night rolls around, the streetlights come on, and still no sign of the girls. Panic sets in. Tootie had called Chan, the karate teacher. There was no sign of Quianna, she never showed up for class. Tootie is now in complete distress and praying, "Lord where is my child?" Boots came from the alley yelling, "Tootie come here!"

"Not now Boots!"

"It's about Quianna. I saw that boy at the store talking to her."

"What boy?"

"Tony's nephew. Ask him if he seen her." She replied, "I will, Boots thanks. Where's he at?" Boots proceeds to tell her that he works with his uncle at the store. She got up and said, "Well I can ask him if he's seen her."

Tootie walked over to the store to ask Rico if he had seen Quianna. But Rico, cunningly, replied, "No, I don't even know the girl."

Just as he was finishing his sentence, Boots walked in the store and said, "You're a damn liar! I saw you out back with Quianna." Rico starts getting upset and says, "Man, get the hell out of here, your ass was imagining that. You probably were drunk and dreamed that shit." Boots tried to grab Rico but Tootie held him back. Listening to the altercation, Mr. Tony yelled, "Hey cut it out" as he gave Rico a hard stare in disappointment. Boots and Tootie left the store and headed back to the stoop. Tootie sat down, gathering her thoughts, and asked Boots, "Why didn't you tell me you saw Quianna with him? What, exactly, were they doing?"

"He got her phone number, and he was trying to hug her. He probably would have tried more if I hadn't kicked the can across the alley." Boots stayed quiet, regretting not having warned Quianna better. It's 8 pm and still no sign of the girls. Renee called the police, they needed help. Meanwhile, in her room, Te'nah cannot get Nia's face out of her head. She can't help thinking that they all ran away with those fine Puerto Rican brothers. She didn't think any of them were having any problems at home, not enough to run away. Te'nah was baffled. She thought to herself, 'I can't mention that I saw them. I will spend my days in the police department. They are probably having a ball.' She snickers. After 15 minutes of mixed thoughts, Te'nah said out loud, "Yeah, I'm not snitching. Nope!" She watched the commotion outside, as the police went by Mr. Tony's store.

Then she got off her bed and headed over there, looking through the window before entering. As she walked in, she was looking for Rico to see if he's the guy from the store and the one the girls were with.

Detective Malone was already in the store questioning Mr. Tony. "Do you have any employees?" "Yes," said Mr. Tony, "my nephew Rico. Rico!" He comes out from the back room. "Oh hey," looks at the detective unexpectedly.

"Hello, Rico is it?"

"Yes, what's wrong officer?"

"We have three missing girls, and we'd like to know if you've seen them."

"Oh no! I haven't."

"Oh, so you do know what girls we're talking about?" Rico hesitantly answers, "No."

"Well, then why did you say, 'oh no' so suddenly, like that?"

Rico starts sweating as he looks off to the side and replied nervously, "I don't know. Umm. Who are these girls?" Detective Malone stared at him, trying to determine his level of involvement with the girls, and says, "Here's a picture of them. Have you ever seen them come in here before? Do you know them?"

Rico admits, "Yes. Yes, I've seen them before. I've only been here a short time, but I've seen them in here before. But I don't know them personally. Like, we've never hung out or anything." Te'nah was in the store by the freezer and watched the interview at the counter with the detective and Rico. She stared Rico down, knowing in her gut he was lying. Detective Malone wasn't convinced either. He instructed them to call him if they recalled anything but decided to keep Rico on his radar.

At the Blue House

A few other girls enter the room where Quianna, Sheeka, and Nia are being held. They warn Quianna, Sheeka and Nia that they are there to stay and that they better listen, or they will get punished. The girls are half naked, hungry, and scared. Quianna asked, "Wait, what's going on? All I can remember is taking a ride with Rico and some guys and I ended up here! What's going on?! Why are we here? I want to leave! Please! I want to go home!" She starts crying very loudly. Suddenly, this guy named Quinn comes in the room and starts yelling, "Shut up! Shut up! This is how it's gonna be. We are going to give you those bathing suits and some heels. Put them on…now! You're gonna do a video."

"These girls here will tell you what to do! Listen to them," Quinn pointed to the group of girls who had walked in earlier. But Quianna insisted, "I want to go home. Where's Rico?" Quinn answered, "Rico is far away, little girl." He grabs Quianna's hair and puts his face close to hers, then breathes on her neck. "You're not going anywhere!" She doesn't move. Then she kicks the back of his leg and he goes down, still holding her hair. He, quickly, regains composure and punches her repeatedly in her head never touching her face, until she passes out. Nia whimpering in the corner, frantically says, "I knew it! I knew it! I should have gone to school."

Sheeka turned to the white girl named Carmen who is seventeen and considered the "bottom-bitch" and asked, "He wants us to do a video?" Carmen answered, "Yeah, they make you do a video first, then you take your clothes off." Sheeka turned away, terrified at the thought.

About 20 minutes later, Quianna regains consciousness. She complained, "My head hurts. I'm going to kill Rico. Why would he let those guys take us without him?" Carmen stopped her,

"Rico is a part of this. He set you up." Quianna was shocked at what she just heard, and yelled, "What?!" Seeing their naivety, Carmen starts advising them, "Listen, you can't get out of this; just do what they tell you! I'm serious. They will beat you and chain you up until you do what they say. Just do it. Okay? It will save you from getting beat."

Quianna asked, "So what is it they want us to do?"

Carmen responded as she stared at the ceiling, "Have sex with men, dance at clubs or escorting. Whatever they want." Quianna cried, "I'm not doing that! This is a dream!! This is just a really bad dream! Body wake up please! Please wake up!" Sheeka, devastated and sobbing uncontrollably utters, "This is all my fault! I'm so sorry ya'll. I'm sorry! I did this." She kept mumbling those words as she rocked back and forth.

"Where's my cell phone?" asked Nia. Carmen answered, "They probably took it. Come on girls let's get you dressed. They'll be coming for you shortly. And you don't want to make them mad."

After the girls get dressed, a tall, tan, and muscular man with a goatee comes into the room. His name is Tino. He looked at the girls and then over at Sheeka, "You're first." Sheeka protested, "Where are you taking me?" Tino shoved her and says, "Don't worry about it, just go!" Sheeka screamed, "No!!! Let me go!" As she fights to stay there. Tino kept pulling her until she released her grip from the door. The girls scream and cry "No!" Carmen and the other girls are sent out leaving Quianna and Nia in the room by themselves. Sheeka is given something to eat, tuna on a hard roll and orange juice. Sheeka's afraid to accept anything from them, but she's starving; she hadn't eaten since early that morning. So, she consumes the food and drink. Once again she becomes woozy and they remove her clothes. They put lingerie on her and place her in different positions as they take pictures and video clips.

Next, they come for Nia. They do the same with her. Finally, they come for Quianna, but she refused to drink the orange juice. Tino came over to her and punched her in the side, which buckled her. Tino yells, "Drink the damn orange juice!" She drinks the juice and becomes under the influence. After the photo shoot they took Sheeka to another room and lay her down on the bed. This room wasn't like the other one they had been in. It was nicely decorated with modern furniture and a beautiful sparkling chandelier over a large marble dinner table. Several men come into the room and look at her in lingerie as if she was a piece of meat on the slaughterhouse table. Lust filled their eyes. Three different men bid on her, one with a heavy European accent. Then they brought out Quianna. She was placed on the dining room table. Six men bid on her, but a Caucasian man from California with wavy silver hair won the auction and she was shipped off with him. Finally, Nia was brought in the room. The men looked but no one bid on her, so she was sent back. Sheeka was set up and ready to be shipped out to her destination in Atlanta, G.A. Tino went into the old dingy room with Nia, angry that she wasn't bid on, he beat her up because she wasn't sold. Then he raped her. Nia laid there, lifeless, tears rolling down her cheek; she closed her eyes tight as she tried her best to imagine herself back home.

They separate the girls and, about an hour later, two more men show up to see the girls. Nia and four white girls are lined up against a light blue wall. One guy picked Nia and another white girl. The other guy takes the other three girls. Nia was headed to New York City with the man who purchased her. Quianna's destination was Los Angeles, but she wasn't leaving until morning. They guys still needed to make her fake ID. Now the girls were all separated so they didn't have each other to rely on. They were scared and unsure of what would happen to them.

The phone rang, and it was Rico on the line. He asked, "How's everything going?" Dom, Tino's brother, laughs, "Fine except for that big one. She nearly took Quinn out!" They both laughed. Rico informed him, "I'll be back tomorrow for a few hours. I'll get them straight." Dom explained, "No need, they've been shipped out."

"What? To where?"

"The big girl, Quianna is going to Los Angeles. Sheeka went to Atlanta, I'm catching the next flight out. And Nia's headed to New York City where Tino can keep an eye on her."

"Wow! Well the police and mothers are asking questions, and this bum tried to fight me at the store. He saw me with the big one, Quianna."

"We might have to take him out if he gives you anymore trouble."

Later that night, Kat drove up to New York City to do her drug pickup on 42nd St. between 8th & 11th. As she parked her car, a white van was at the light going in the opposite direction. Kat gets out of her car and sees Nia in the window, and they lock eyes. Nia put her hands on the window in desperation, trying to mouth the words 'Help me,' without getting caught. Kat was perplexed as she sees Nia. She got back in her car and starts it up again to go after her. Traffic begins moving and the van goes with the traffic. Kat waited to pull off, but it was too late, she had lost Nia and the van. Kat pulled her car over and started crying.

She wanted to call the police, but she was hesitant. She struggled with the thought of bringing attention to herself with her illegal activities but still thought she should help this little girl. After a few minutes of going back and forth, she chose selfishly and decided to say nothing. Even though she was feeling overwhelmed with guilt, she preferred living with this secret. She returned to make her pickup and headed back across the Lincoln Tunnel to Newark.

Chapter 6

Rico and the Young Girls

It's been four days since the girls disappeared, and back at the bodega, Mr. Tony is feeling confused. Something just wasn't right, and he couldn't put his finger on it. He was torn between his feelings about these young girls disappearing and his nephew's behavior the other night with Boots. He watched them grow up, and he was seriously hoping his nephew had nothing to do with their disappearance. As the customers came in and out of the store, talking about the whereabouts of the girls, Mr. Tony noticed Boots had positioned himself outside the bodega. In all the years that he's been there, Boots had never done this before. He walked outside the store to talk to him and says, "Hey Boots, how are you? I noticed you keep looking through the window, are you okay? You need something to eat? I can have Rico fix you up something."

Boots sarcastically replied, "I don't need nothing from Rico, he's done enough!"

"What do you mean?"

"I saw him messing with those girls, I know he's got something to do with them being missing."

Mr. Tony started getting agitated, "Don't go making accusations like that Boots if you don't have any proof! My nephew is no saint, but he's no kidnapper either!"

Boots yelled back, "Your nephew is no good! Tony, that boy ain't right...you'll see! Don't put your money on him, cause you're gonna lose!"

Mr. Tony walked away and headed back into the store. He looked at Rico knowing that Boots might be telling the truth. He thinks back to before the girls were missing. First thing he remembered was Rico missing from the store, then seeing him on the security video with Quianna. He thought back to the day they went missing and Rico wasn't at the house when it was time to go to work. He showed up late that day and, when the detective came by with questions, Rico claimed he didn't even know the girls. He started thinking that Rico might be up to his old tricks. He brought him to New Jersey because he was hanging out with some bad dudes in Puerto Rico who were connected in the sex trafficking ring. There's no way he could be doing that here because he didn't know anyone, or so he thought.

On Saturday, Rico got off work and headed to the pool hall. He found Larry there with visible scars and scratches to his face and ears. Rico looked at him and said, "Damn man, where you been? What happened to you? I came to check you out for that hookup with the interview." Larry replied, "Yeah I didn't even check into that yet. I've been preoccupied with trying to kick this guy's ass, but I can't find him!"

"Who is he?"

"Nobody. Forget it. What you been up to?"

"I'm going to New York tonight."

"Will you be staying or coming right back?"

Rico answered, "I'm going to the club to check out some honeys and handle some business. You want to go?" Larry replied, "Yeah, what time?" "In about an hour, can you drive?" Larry agreed.

Two hours passed, Larry and Rico headed to the city. They arrived at the gentlemen's club, sat by the bar and ordered drinks. Larry was surprised by how the bouncer and the bar tender seemed extra courteous with Rico. But he quickly dismissed that thought as he guzzled down his beer. Meanwhile in the back, Nia waited in the girl's make up room. It was her first time on stage. She was only five feet tall, about 90 pounds but the lead dancer, Carmen, coached her on how to perform on stage and gave her a drink and Ecstasy to make her relax. The DJ announced the next dancer's name: 'Innocent'. She was rocking a blonde bob cut wig with a lot of makeup. She looked like she was in her late teens. She came out grooving to the music, dancing all provocatively; numb to anything else she might have been feeling.

Larry looked up at the girl on stage and said to himself, 'Damn, she looks familiar.' But he couldn't place where he might have seen her before. No longer paying any attention to her dancing, Larry couldn't take his eyes off her face. He was trying really hard to remember where he knew her from and leans over to Rico to say, "She looks so familiar - I know her from somewhere." Rico swallowed the rest of his drink hard, reached into his wallet, and threw a tip on the bar counter. Completely dismissing Larry's comment, he taps Larry on the arm and says, "Let's go to the next spot." So, they leave.

Back in the neighborhood, Reverend Briggs is having an all-night prayer vigil for the missing girls. Everyone met up at the church. They were told to wear something comfortable since this was a shut in (all night) service. Breakfast would be served in the morning, but prayer would last all night. Prayer began at midnight until 6 am Sunday morning. That morning church started at the usual time. The mother of the church, Mother Morton prays, "God touch the hearts of whoever has these children. Release them now in the name of Jesus! Reverse the agenda of the enemy and God be a fortress for them. Change the hearts of the girls. If they ran away, bring them back home now in the name of Jesus."

Bett and Monster, Jean and Boots attended the Shut In. Te'nah comes over and sits next to her mom, hoping that the service would relieve some of the guilt she's been carrying.

In Mr. Tony's apartment, he's struggling to sleep so he goes downstairs to the store and enters the back room. He rolls the tape back to the first day of Rico's arrival. Not only does the store camera capture surveillance of the front of the store, but it also captures activity in the back alleyway. Good thing he only gave the detective the tapes he asked for and not all of them. As he's fast forwarding through the tape, he sees Quianna and Rico together several times. At one point, he saw them in an embrace and Rico was kissing her face. He also sees Rico giving the little girls who hang with Sheeka and Nia some money. He fast forwards some more and sees a blue van with what looks like Rico in the passenger side. He rewinds repeatedly and to his amazement, "It's his other nephews, Aponte and Quinn. Aponte was the ringleader of the Trafficking Ring in Puerto Rico.

Mr. Tony screamed, "Dios mio!" He held his head and started to cry. 'Rico kidnapped those girls? Ay Dios mio! This can't be. What have I done?' Mr. Tony went back to his apartment above the store. He paced back and forth, replaying the images he had seen, and then went into Rico's room to rummage through his things.

Not knowing what he was searching for, he finds airline receipts for the four guys that came from Puerto Rico. He also found a Money Gram receipt from Puerto Rico to New Jersey for $2,000 sent to Rico one week before their arrival. Realizing the evidence he had in his hands, he was torn and didn't know what to do. This is his sister's only son; if he turns Rico in, he will hurt her dearly. Aponte is his brother's oldest son who has always been trouble, a lost cause. But he was mostly confused about seeing Quinn with them.

Meanwhile, Rex got a call from work to come in, everyone is on call. He headed in to work but called Larry to tell him they needed him to come in too. Larry replied, "I can't make it today, I'm in New York." Rex hung up, shaking his head and clocked in for work. The guys come home from the city just before dawn. Over in Atlanta, Sheeka arrived at the airport, sad and scared. She had been coached throughout the entire trip and was given drugs to relax. The man who bid on her ordered his assistant to send Sheeka to the massage parlor. There she was taught the art of massage and was told she would sleep where she works, on top of a massage table. Aponte sent Dom to oversee her and warned her that if she is caught talking to her client, she would be beaten on the spot and her family would be tortured because of her betrayal.

Dom gave Sheeka Oxycontin and told her to get herself together because she had a guest coming to her room. She's numb to any pain as her first client walks through the door of the room. It's an older Pakistani man, medium build, with grey hair and a devilish smile. He starts feeling her up and down, but she gains control by laying him on the table. She is so high off the pills that she is completely disconnected from reality. She completes her first sale with this man; and, when he leaves, she is told to clean up so she can entertain her next guest.

On a large private jet, Quianna is on flight to Los Angeles. She was told pretty much the same as

Sheeka; if she brought any attention to them, her family would be killed. To show her they were serious, they recited her mother's name and address and even mentioned her workplace. Of all three, she was the only one they were worried about because she is the strong and bull-headed one. Worried for her mom's safety, she agreed to follow all their requests and was prepped to be an escort. Out of all the girls, she was also the prettiest with the most matured body for her age. Quianna is placed in a luxury apartment in the hills of the San Fernando Valley. Though hard to imagine, she had gotten the best of this terrible life. Quinn was assigned to her as her limo driver. He always carries a gun on his side making her aware of who's in charge. He gave Quianna Hennessey and heroin to relax and perform her work. She was taken to high rise apartments, hotel suites, and penthouses; and did whatever was required. Her only motivation was keeping her mother safe back home, disregarding even her own life.

Chapter 7

Raid at the Blue Diamond

Two months passed by; Vivian and Renee were at their wits' end. In all this time, they had been doing TV interviews and talking to reporters. Their faces were plastered on the front of every newspaper, pleading for someone to come forward with any information. They constantly checked in with Det. Malone. The moms refused to lose hope, someone somewhere knew something about their daughters.

Shae had the nerve to contact Larry, out of the blue. He answered her call and asked her to meet him in the park. Shae agrees, of course. An hour passes, and Larry bought a newspaper as he waited for Shae to get to the park. The headline of the front page read *Two Months & No Signs of the 3 Missing Girls*, their pictures just beneath. He stares at the article and recognizes the one girl Nia from the club. Shae arrived and hugged Larry intensely, and they kiss. Larry starts apologizing to her and tells her that he didn't know what had come over him that day. "It won't ever happen again. I couldn't sleep. All I could do was think about you. I didn't want to call you because I didn't know how you'd feel towards me. Baby, it will never happen again," he promised, adding, "Did you press charges?"

Shae listened quietly and waited until he was done talking before answering him, "No I didn't. How could I? I love you! I missed you, I thought maybe you had moved on."

"What? Baby I couldn't get you off my mind. You were all I thought about, no one else. So…what have you been up to…away from me?"

"Nothing. Really. Recovering…and praying for the girls in my building to be found, I just can't believe…" she stopped as she looks at the paper Larry is holding. She then tells him, "Wait. Those are the girls in my building." She points at the paper. He starts to say something, "I've seen..." then he abruptly stops talking. Puzzled, Shae asks, "What was that?" Larry shakes his head to disregard his words and says nothing more about the girls. Then, he grabbed her hand and they strolled through the park.

It's Saturday afternoon and Mr. Tony is still reliving the scenes from his security tape, but he had decided that night that he was not going to say anything, and he would just watch Rico for more evidence instead. Rico was at work, and when lunch time came, he snuck out to the back alley. Mr. Tony saw him talking to two little girls, again giving them money. Just like he had before. Mr. Tony ran to the front of the store as Rico came in. The girls entered the store and spoke to Rico like it was their first time seeing him that day. Then, they bought something to drink with the money he had just given them. Confused, Mr. Tony is watching this play out. He looked over at the door and sees Boots. He knew exactly what Boots was thinking, as he stood there like a sidewalk guard. 'If he did get the other girls, he won't get these two!' Mr. Tony nervously waved at Boots, but he ignored him, still mad from their last conversation. The girls left the store, Rico went back to his work, and Boots had retreated back into his alley.

About an hour later, Larry called Rico. "What's up man?" Rico answered, "Just work. What's up?" Larry asked, "What time do you get off?" "Five-thirty, why - what's up?" Larry tells him to come by the pool hall, so Rico agrees to meet him. Rico hung up, and Te'nah enters the store. Rico tried to serve her, but she walks away from him and goes directly to Mr. Tony to be served. Once Mr. Tony gave her the food and took her money, she stared Rico down and as she left, she said, "You're going to get yours!" Rico laughed nervously, playing coy in front of his uncle, he was not sure of what she knew but took her very seriously.

Mr. Tony watched Te'nah's reaction to Rico, more confirmation. Boots, standing in front again, stopped her outside of the store and said, "Girl, you know something, what is it? That boy got something to do with them missing girls?" Boots knew he had to get Te'nah to talk, so he tells her what he saw to persuade her to trust him. She pauses for a moment, she has always been able to confide in Boots, so she finally decided to tell him about that dreadful day.

Meanwhile at the church...Reverend Briggs pleads with God for the girls to come home safely. "Set the captives free God. Lord, touch the hearts of them that hold our children. Save our children, Lord, we rebuke the hand of the enemy now in the name of Jesus. Release your hold Satan now in the name of Jesus! Bring them home, Father."

After the altercation at the club, Blue had to relocate for a minute, so he went to New York to work at a Gentlemen's Club in Hell's Kitchen. He begins to look around the venue and get familiar with the new location as he starts filling out the paperwork in the office when he hears a familiar voice. He disregarded it because he didn't know anyone there. In the midst of his concentration, the girls must come and sign new contracts for tax purposes. So, one by one, they sign and leave. He glances up from time to time, not thinking much of it.

Nia comes in the office and she and Blue lock eyes. Blue freezes, with tears in his eyes, he was about to scream her name, but she quickly put her finger up to her mouth to hush him. She came close to him and whispered in his ear, "Get me out of here!" Blue shook his head in agreement, "Okay, let me finish this paperwork. Act normal! I will get you out of here!" Nia warned Blue, "Watch out for the big guy, Tino, he's watching me." She sighed and walked out of the office, now with an ounce of hope in her heart. Blue took a break for a couple of hours before starting at the club and headed to the Midtown Manhattan Police Station. He sat down to talk with Detective Rouse, a medium height African American man with a "no-nonsense" mug on his face.

Two hours later, the girls prepare as they have a show to put on. Blue goes back to the establishment just to make sure he has eyes on Nia. But when he gets there, he can't find her. He starts panicking and looking for her frantically. When she came out of the bathroom and he saw her, he was relieved. They glanced at each other as she passed by him, both with a slight smirk on their faces. Nia got in the lineup for her upcoming dance. The late afternoon crowd was bigger than usual. The DJ introduced "Innocent" and Nia starts her performance. After about 10 minutes, Blue grabbed his phone to make the call, the place is surrounded, and cops start charging in. Everybody gets down, including Nia! One of the cops grabs Nia, assuring her she was now safe and escorts Nia outside. Finally, she had been found!

Waiting outside, Blue ran over to her and they cried in each other's arms. Nia sobbed, "I've been praying, praying for this…how is my mom? Is she okay" "She's been trying to hold it together, all worried about you. It's been a lot on her. Let me call her." Blue pulled out his phone to call Renee. Just then an FBI agent stopped Blue, "Excuse me, sir. I have to ask you to hold off on that call. We will let you make a call to your mother, but first we have some questions for you for our investigation." Everyone in the club was hauled off to the police station.

Back in Newark, Rico met up with Larry at the pool hall. They shot one game of pool and Larry asked Rico, "Remember when I had said that the girl at the club looked familiar?" Rico, wondering where this was going, answered, "Yeah." Larry slaps the newspaper on the table and points to Nia.

"No way! You know her?" Rico hollered with surprise in his voice. Larry, looking at Rico suspiciously, shot back "Yeah, and you should too! She comes into your store. Quite often. She lives 200 feet from your Uncle's place."

Rico answered, "Bro...I didn't recognize her with all that makeup on, and you know I haven't been working there long!" Larry agrees, "Yeah. That's right." Right then, that stopped Larry's suspicion of Rico as he concluded, 'He might be right. He has only been here for a short time.' The topic of Nia ended, and they went back to their game.

Detective Rouse took Nia and Blue back to the station to question her. Nia was becoming extremely impatient as she was coming down off her high, with all the excitement going on. She just wanted to call her mom! So much time had passed, so many days away from her, she missed her mother desperately. The thought of being able to be back home made her anxious. Detective Rouse asked, "Where have you been, why did you run away?" Nia replied in disbelief, "I didn't run away! I was kidnapped!"

"Kidnapped?"

"Yes! These men kidnapped me and my friends."

"What men? Where were you?"

"We were by the school. They picked us up in New Jersey. In Newark."

"You got in their car?"

"They were friends of Rico."

"Rico? Who is Rico?"

"Yes, Rico is Mr. Tony's nephew at the corner store. By my house. Tony's Bodega."

"Okay. Did he ask you if you needed a ride?"

Nia stated, "No, he said we were going to Coney Island but then he kidnapped us. He took us somewhere, drugged, and raped us." Now, Nia is crying as she recalled everything she's lived in the past months.

"Who else was with you and who were the other men?"

"I want to call my mom."

"I understand, Nia. Just a few more questions, then I'll let you call."

"No, I want to call her now! I'll answer your questions after I speak with her." Seeing how upset she was, the detective finally backed off and said, "Okay, okay, Nia. Let's go ahead and call your mom." He picks up the phone from his desk and hands the receiver over to her. While Nia made her call, another detective questioned Blue in a different room. Detective Brown, a short and thin white woman with short brown hair, stared at Blue quietly before asking, "How do you know the young lady?"

"I've known her since she was born. We live in the same building in Newark."

"Are you the owner of the Blue Diamond Gentleman's Club?"

"No, I was just supposed to start managing there."

"What did she say to you when she saw you?"

"All she said was 'Watch out for the big guy outside because he's watching.' I'm the one who called you guys! I called Detective Rouse. He set all of this up. Ask him! I've done my part. Now I'd like to see Nia! Make sure she's alright"

Detective Brown tells Blue "Sir, I'm sorry, I can't do that. I have to be sure you're not one of the captors."

"Ask Detective Rouse, why would I call you if I captured her ass?" Now Blue was getting angry.

He threw his hands in the air then slammed them on the table in front of him.

While he's talking to the detective, Nia is on the phone with her mother. As soon as she heard her mother's voice answer, she began to cry. She could barely get a 'Hello' out. "Nia! Oh my God, Nia? Is that you, baby girl?"

"Yes, mom, it's me. Mom, I missed you so much! Please come to New York, please come and get me! I'm at the police station! They'll give you all the information you need! Please hurry mom! Please! Here's the detective. His name is Detective Rouse."

Detective Rouse gave Renee the directions and the information she needed. Renee asked him, "Do you want me to tell the other mothers to come and get their girls?" The detective responded, "Other moms? We only have Nia ma'am, I'm not sure of what other moms or girls there are." Renee exclaimed, "Oh no! No. How did you find her? How did you find Nia?"

"The club manager found her. His name is Blue, I believe. He came down to the precinct. We're questioning him right now. Ma'am, we have to finish our investigation, but we'll see you when you get here." Renee hurried off the phone, crying while praising God that her daughter was alive. She left to Tootie's house and tells her that they found Nia, but she was by herself. Renee asked Tootie if she wanted to go with her to the precinct. She was happy for Renee but after hearing that her daughter wasn't rescued, she declined in disappointment. After she left Tootie's, Renee went to Vivian's to give her the news. "I'm going to the precinct in the city - do you want to come?" Vivian explained, "No, I don't have a babysitter." She was sad that her daughter was not rescued either.

Renee glanced at her watch, it's 6:15 pm. She told Vivian she'd get all the information she could about Sheeka. Renee left the building and ran to Reverend Briggs, crying. "Reverend, they found my baby!!" Mr. Willie wrapped his arms around them both and they all begin to praise God together. As they come away from the huddle, they see Tootie standing on the sidewalk looking worried with her head down and both hands together. Reverend Briggs called over to her, "Tootie, you better come celebrate with Renee! What God makes happen for others, He will make happen for you! Praise God with her, so your daughter will be found." Reverend Briggs then lets out a thunderous, "Hallelujah! Praise you Jesus!"

The street starts buzzing about Nia being found. Ricky went to Mr. Tony's store and tells Rico that the girl Nia has been found as he buys a pack of cigarettes and then leaves. Rico started sweating when he heard the news. He goes to the back of the store to tell his Uncle he's leaving, never mentioning that Nia was rescued. As soon as Rico leaves he calls his contact Tino but gets no answer. Tino had been arrested with the rest of the club management. He tries a couple more times, then calls Dom, who answered, "What's up Rico?"

"Yo, I just heard they found Nia, the young girl in New York. I called Tino and he isn't answering!"

"What? Hold up, I'll try him, but I haven't heard anything. I'll call him now!" They hung up. Dom called Tino and it went straight to voicemail. He then calls Quinn. Quinn answered, "Yeah man. What's good?"

"I just heard Tino lost his girl, the young one - she's back home!"

"What?! Oh shit! He's so stupid! We should have kept him at the house! Damn! Aponte is gonna be pissed. And, you already know who else is gonna hear about this. Who told you?"

"Rico heard it on the street!"

"I'll call Rico now!" Quinn ended the call and dialed Rico's number. "Rico, what happened?" He replied, "I heard Nia was found, that's all I know, and I can't get in touch with Tino!"

"You need to leave right now or our whole operation is over!"

"Okay, let me get my bag and I'm out." Quinn advised him, "Just go to Albany until I call for you!" Rico grabbed a pre-packed duffle bag he kept behind the store and caught a bus to Grand Central Station in New York, heading to Albany, NY

Now Boots got the word that Nia was found, so he headed to Mr. Tony's to tell him. "Tony, where's your nephew?"

"He just left, why? He didn't say where."

"Yeah, well, I don't think he's coming back!" Boots shook his head in disgust. If Boots was right, then Rico definitely had something to do with it. Mr. Tony may never see Rico again. Boots stormed back out of the store.

Chapter 8

The Search for Rico

Mr. Tony walked behind the counter and calls Rico, but the call goes straight to voicemail. Fearing all his suspicions were right, he left a message.

Earlier that day, notices had been sent out to tenants concerning the renovations which would start tomorrow. Tootie and Shae had planned on staying at a hotel because their apartments were being worked on first. Shae was ready for a change. Bett and Monster grabbed their things along with some of Blue's items. Tootie was working doubles and hadn't had a chance to grab anything from the apartment to take to the hotel by tomorrow. So she just grabbed a few outfits and uniforms, hoping it would be enough.

Back in L.A., Quinn had just finished talking to Aponte, he realizes that he must tighten up his operation. Aponte warned Quinn to watch Quianna like a hawk, otherwise the next call would be from "el Jefe" (the boss). Her next client was a winery owner. He requested Quianna three times a week. To prevent any further incidents, Quinn walks up to Quianna, puts a gun to her back, and pushes her hard! "Remember what I told you! Your mother won't feel a thing, believe me! No mess-ups! You have a client tonight."

Quianna questioned, "With who?"

"The vineyard client at 9:00 pm. Just make sure you're ready."

"Well, I'm not doing anything now. Why don't you come chill with me?" As she runs her fingers down his chest. He looked at Quianna, edging closer and tempted to take her up on the offer, but quickly regains his composure. He started thinking about Tino's mishap. Quianna says, "I'll fix you something to eat. We can chill and watch a movie. I have 3 hours to kill. Come on Quinn?" Not seeing the harm in hanging out, he flops on the couch.

Quianna put on a movie and popped a bag of popcorn. Sitting close to Quinn with her skin touching his. She took every opportunity to move closer and closer to him, pressing against him. Then he put his arm over the couch as if he wanted to hug her. Quianna didn't wait any longer, she reached over and started kissing him. He fell under her spell; they begin taking several articles of clothing off as they kissed passionately, walking backward toward the bedroom. They fall back on the bed and begin to fondle each other, which leads to sex. Quinn couldn't hold back his feelings. He was falling for Quianna. They both laid there on her white crisp, 1500 thread count Egyptian Cotton sheets with fluffy white goose pillows.

He falls asleep shortly after. Her plan had worked however, she was physically attracted to his fine Puerto Rican ass. She thought back to the conversation with Boots while staring at the ceiling. He had told her that he had a bad feeling about Rico. 'He was right, I should have listened,' she got lost in her thoughts.

In New Jersey, the Newark police and Detective Malone were contacted, and a warrant was issued for Rico Mercado's arrest. The NPD went to Mr. Tony's Bodega, but it was closed for the day. The police rang the bell to his apartment upstairs and asked him to come down to the station. They asked if Rico was there with him? He replied, "No, he isn't. What's this about?"

"You will find out once you get to the station. We need you to come with us."

In Atlanta, Sheeka had been trained to give massages, but probably wouldn't be doing it for long. It was only a cover up for a brothel. Dom told her that her family would never be seen again if she didn't comply. During her time there, she tried to get out through a bathroom window but was caught by the nail salon owner, next door. They beat and drugged her, making her work more hours for her disloyalty. They told her that, if she got caught by the police, she would be locked up for prostitution.

Sheeka stuck out like a sore thumb being a black girl in a predominantly Asian area of Atlanta. Asian men fantasized about being with black women. She realized, in her moment of sobriety, that she had to make this work for her. She needed to make a way to escape. In her moments alone, she prayed, "Lord, please help me. I need you now!" She was able to get her nails done at the salon next door and struck up a conversation with the nail tech. While her feet and hands were drying, the tech went outside to smoke a cigarette. While she's out, Sheeka steals her phone and leaves.

Dom saw Sheeka enter the massage parlor and tells her to hurry up, she has a client coming soon. She goes into the bathroom and turns on the shower. With the water on, she takes advantage of the noise and calls home. Her brother, Buddy, answered. He was so excited to hear from her, but she quickly tells him to put mommy on the phone. Outside, she can hear Dom's voice. Her brother was taking too long, and she ended the call. She cut the phone off and hid it behind the toilet, in between it and the wall.

The FBI arrived at the precinct as they were now handling Nia's case. The NYPD has a briefing with the police officers and detectives to bring the FBI agents up to speed. Special Agent Wilson conducts the meeting on Human Trafficking and Sex Trafficking. He explains that Human Trafficking is modern day slavery. People are smuggled, traded, and used as objects. Some are tricked into believing that if they came to the U.S., they would have a better life; and, once here, they are forced into prostitution. Agent Wilson continued, "There is also forced labor. These people are forced to work for very little. They are beaten or sold as property. There is a chance that the food we eat everyday has been picked or fixed by someone who is a human slave. The clothes we wear and laptops you use have probably been handled or made by a human slave. I want to familiarize you with Human and Sex Trafficking victims. They are usually young, as young as 12 years old. They are impressionable and they are scared. They are away from their families and are told that, if they try to leave, they will be killed, or their families hurt. Some are starved and made to stay up long hours as punishment."

Everyone in the department is listening intently as he goes on, "We need every officer that arrests a prostitute or young person who is dislocated from their families to ask a barrage of questions. These traffickers need to be stopped! This is a multi-million-dollar business. This is much larger than what occurred here last night. Which is why we're here. Families are being hurt. Lives are being destroyed over greed. Officers…just think of it as if someone took your own daughter or son, niece, or nephew. Make it personal - get someone's child back home to them. Save a life today."

"What are the signs? How can we verify it's a trafficking situation?" One officer questioned.

Wilson answered, "Multiple people in a cramped space. For instance, you pull over a truck with a dozen or more people in it. Typically these people live with their employers. Or if you're unable to speak with them without the employer present. Poor living conditions. If the person seems submissive or fearful; you should definitely look for signs of physical abuse." Everyone left the conference room and started working on their leads.

A few days passed and it's now Monday around twelve thirty-five p.m. and Ronnie and Ricky are on their grind on the block slinging dope as usual. Ricky was upset about Quianna. He didn't understand how only one of the girls could've turned up. So he starts questioning his customers asking if they had heard anything and telling them to keep their ears out for any information. He promises a reward for their help.

When Mr. Tony had gone down to the station, they questioned him intensely, especially considering Rico was his nephew. But they were satisfied with the interrogation and that he had no knowledge of the kidnappings or his nephew's whereabouts. He offered to give up all the store video tapes as well.

The Newark police swarmed the neighborhood. The detectives were now more determined than ever to find the other girls. There were about 10 cop cars at least. The officers were going from house to house questioning people about the whereabouts of these young girls. Officer Miller and her partner went to Mr. Tony's bodega to check out the tape. She asked Mr. Tony, "Who are these little girls that Rico is talking to in the alley?" These were the 2 little girls who often played with Sheeka and Nia. Mr. Tony tells her, "They live in the building over there," pointing across the street. Officer Miller leaves while her partner finishes reviewing the tape. She heads over to the "Bricks" to find the little girls and asks both their mothers for permission to speak with them. They both reply, "Yes, of course."

Directing the conversation at the girls, she said, "Hi I'm Officer Miller. I know that you are good friends with the young ladies who are missing. I saw the video tape from Mr. Tony's store and you're both talking to the young man, Rico. He seems really friendly. Why did he give you money?"

The first girl, Joy, answers "To buy something out of the store." The second girl, Lisha, says "To put some money in our pockets so we won't be broke." "Did he ever ask you to go with him anywhere or do anything with him?" The girls grow silent...then Lisha says, "I'm no snitch!" Her mother turned to her, "You better tell her everything you know, Lisha! What do you mean, you're not a snitch? Your friends are missing!" Joy's mother gives her the 'look' and she started spilling her guts! "He told me he could buy me whatever I wanted, and I wouldn't have to ask my mother for anything. I could just ask him." Lisha chimed in, "He told me I was pretty, and I had a nice body. He said when I got older that all the guys would want me. But that he'd protect me from the bad ones." Lisha's mother said, "Who the hell is this guy? I got some shit to say to him myself! Let me find his ass first! Damn Pervert!"

Officer Miller continues her conversation with the girls, "Do you know how to get in touch with Rico? We need to ask him if he's seen Quianna or Sheeka. We found Nia!" The girls were excited to hear this and asked, "When is she coming home?"

"Soon, but first we need Rico to help us find the other girls. Do you have a way of getting in touch with him?" The girls are quiet again. Joy looked at her mom as she pulled out a cell phone that Rico had bought her. She gives it to the officer as her mom looks at her in shock. Officer Miller took the phone and called Rico. After 2 rings, Rico answered, "Hey baby girl!" "Rico Mercado, this is Officer Miller…" Rico immediately hung up. In a panic, he throws away his prepaid phone and rushes into the house in Albany to use the landline phone and call Quinn.

It was almost 10:00 am in California and Quinn was just waking up as he answered, "Yo." Rico yelled, "The police called my phone, Quinn! One of the young girls must have told them how to find me! I'm here at the house now and I threw that phone away. I'll pick up a new one and call you later with the number." Quinn responded, "Okay, stay low. I'll call the others."

Chapter 9

Quinn and Quianna

After he gets off the phone with Rico, Quinn was concerned about the information he just received. Worried about getting caught but also because he has feelings for Quianna and she knows it. Quianna passed by him and says, "Hey Babe." He just looked at her not knowing what to say. He knew she had feelings for him too, they had both come a long way from their first interaction. But this was too risky considering Quinn was #1 in charge of overseeing the business, after Aponte who is the boss' right hand man in Puerto Rico. He needed to tighten up on security since Rico's cover had clearly been blown. He was having a hard time separating his feelings from the business.

"Would you like something to eat?" Quinn replied, "Yeah, that would be nice," and smiles. She smiled back, grazing her hand across his muscular chest as she leans over him. She gets up to fix breakfast, steak and eggs with watermelon slices on the side. She serves Quinn breakfast in bed as they look into each other's eyes.

"Umm, listen…can I be honest with you?" Quinn looked at her and nodded his head yes. She says, "I'm caught up in this horrible situation. The only thing getting me through this is you, Quinn. I've…I gotta be honest, I caught feelings for you. And I…" Quianna pauses.

"Go ahead. Finish." He is persistent on finding out what else she has to say.

Quianna lets out a sigh, "I look forward to seeing your face after I leave all these men. You make me feel safe. I… you know what, never mind."

"No…wait. What? What is it?"

"I just wish we could be together and just get away from here. Get away from everything. I just think…I would have someone to love me and…and I'd be happy."

Quinn shrugs his shoulders, "You'd go home and just leave me once you saw your family."

"No I wouldn't, truth is it's only me and my mom. She's always working. She never really has time for me. Most of the time, I'm by myself or with my friends. I've just always wanted to be loved. I need to be loved. You know?"

Quinn looked into Quianna's eyes with a passionate glare and then snapped out of it. He shot up off the bed and looked out over the mountain view saying nothing…weighing his options in silence. Quianna left the room not knowing if her charm had worked or if she blew it. Several minutes pass and Quinn gets dressed, mentioning he has to leave. Quianna was now worried and regretting having said anything. Quinn had left without eating his breakfast.

In New Jersey, Boots was questioned by the detectives; he answered all their questions and was very cooperative. After they leave, Boots returns to the alley and he began to pray for the girls to be brought home safely. He heard Kat arguing with someone on the phone from the alley. He can't hear the conversation too good so he goes to the building basement where he can hear everything through the floor vent.

Kat is talking, "Why would you do that so close to home? Why? I begged you! The cops are coming here asking questions. They're everywhere! Which makes it hard for me to run business. I watched those girls grow up. I almost tried to rescue Nia. She doesn't deserve this. Rico, that bastard! Now I can't sell shit. My corners are locked down! I told you to leave his ass over there. He's a player, he's inexperienced and immature."

As Boots is listening to the conversation, he is puzzled and unsure of what he's hearing. He's wondering if his long-time neighbor had something to do with the kidnapping of these children. Boots listened further as Kat's conversation goes on.

"So you're coming in at what time? Where are you staying? You can't stay here…it's too hot!" The person on the other end says, "Okay, I'll be in a hotel in Jamaica, New York." "Ok, which one? I miss you baby. I hate that we have to be apart like this. It's been 2 years. I don't know how much longer I can do this. I'm getting older, you know. And money isn't everything especially if I can't spend it," a disgusted look comes across her face. Boots could only hear someone speaking Spanish. He never knew Kat was bi-lingual. Kat is still talking, "Yeah, I got the hotel set up for the tenants. They will have 2 of the same suites. I rented it for four months, two weeks for each tenant. What time will your guys be here to start? The voice replied, "Eight a.m. Have the realtor call Tootie to be sure that she will be out of the apartment."

She answers back, "Okay, babe. I can't wait to see you! I love you!" Boots was unsure of what he had just heard. He thought silently, 'Wait, Kat is the bilingual landlord of this building and has a Spanish man who kidnapped the kids? Is that it? Nah, this is some bullshit! I must be hearing things.' Guzzling down a forty ounce of Old English, he was still in his thoughts. 'I've known her for at least 10 years! Is she talking about Rico? Nah...I never seen them talk! Maybe I'm wrong. Nah...can't be!' Boots went to the front of the building. Ten minutes later, Kat came out on the steps with a short, strapless fluorescent pink sundress, wearing gold hoop earrings and gold strappy sandals. Kat says, "Hey Boots! Hot day huh?" Boots' voice cracks, "Yeah."

"You seen Jean today?"

"Nah, too many police. I guess they ran her nosey ass out the window." Laughing Boots adds, "They ran them boys off the corner too!" Kat has nothing to say for a minute...then replied, "I guess!"

Kat and Boots both know that she's behind all the drug slinging in the streets. Again in his thoughts, 'Kat's out here selling that shit. Everybody looking, like damn zombies. She's pushing this poison to her own people!'

"Look at her ass," he said out loud as he pointed across the street to this girl. "She looks 50, but is probably only thirty-eight, scratching and nodding out."

Kat dismissed his comment, "Boots, the people are coming to remodel the top floor, so they will be using the alleyway, I'm sure."

"Oh, you know a lot about this, they payin' you to be the building manager or somethin'?" He laughed.

"No, the management company told me about a month ago." Boots knew she was lying. "I heard they were going to a hotel. Is that true?" Never making eye contact with Boots, Kat replied, "Yeah the Suites by the airport."

"They sure are accommodating. And you know everything. They should be paying yo' ass to be the supervisor," he said sarcastically.

Kat's house phone rings. She abruptly runs in and ends her conversation with Boots to answer her phone.

Across the street, Mr. Tony opened his store and noticed there was no sign of Rico all weekend. He hadn't heard from him at all. Mr. Tony called home in Puerto Rico to ask his sister, Maria, if

Rico had returned home or if she had heard from him. He says, "Hola hermana. (Hello sister). Has hablado con tu hijo? (Have you talked to your son)?"

Maria answered, "Porque? Que paso? Donde esta el, Antonio?" (Why? What happened? Where is he?) Tony replied, "La Policia lo esta buscando." (The police are looking for him).

"Que, pero porque?" (What? But why?)

"Alguien secuestro a algunas niñas y quieren interrogarlo." (Someone kidnapped some little girls, and they want to interrogate him).

"O Dios mio." (Oh my God!). As she puts her hands on her head, "Mi pobre bebe (my poor baby). Haz lo que tengas que hacer para salvarlo." (Do whatever you have to do to save him).

"No, Maria. Esta vez no!" (Not this time Maria!) "El tiene que aprender (he has to learn). Lo intente, intente ayudarlo (I tried, I tried helping him). Pero ese muchacho no es bueno, Maria (But that boy is no good, Maria)! Se acabo! (I'm done). El esta por su cuenta (He's on his own). Disculpame, hermana. Lo intente." (Forgive me, sister, I tried).

Crying, Maria begs, "No Antonio, por favor. Te lo suplico!" (No Tony, please. I'm begging you!).

Tony says, "Disculpame. Te quiero, hermana." (Forgive me. I love you sister) and hangs up.

Chapter 10

Sheeka's Story

The weeks continue to pass by. Sheeka and five other young ladies were sent to a massage parlor to do a bachelor party for ten black guys at 1:00 pm. Sheeka was so hungry she started her massage, but she stopped as she started getting nauseous and feeling sick. The young man on the table asked her if she was okay. She told him she was fine, but just hungry. The young man mentions, "Well, they need to give you a lunch break. I'll wait." She answered, "No," with fright in her voice.

"Damn, you don't get a lunch break?"

"No, never mind...it's okay. I'm okay!" She begins his massage again but starts feeling ill again. He sits up this time and says, "Look, I have a sandwich in my bag, you want it?" She replied, "Yes...please!" with desperation. He grabbed a white paper back with grease stains on the side from inside his black duffle bag. The mouth-watering smell of food burst from the bag as he handed her his sandwich and fries. She snatched it out of his hand and savored that first bite.

"Are you okay?"

"Shh…" Sheeka put her finger up to her mouth to signal him to be quiet. She says, "I'm not supposed to be talking!" Suddenly, she starts to cry. In an attempt to console her, the guy says, "Are you okay? Seriously. What's wrong? What's going on here? Are they hurting you?"

Her eyeliner is streaming down her face and she shakes her head. "Yes please, I just want to go home!"

"Okay, calm down. Where do you live? I'll give you a ride home!"

"New Jersey. I live in New Jersey."

"New Jersey?!!"

"Shh…please! You're being too loud! They'll hear you!"

"Wait a minute. How old are you?" Now the guy was taking a good look at Sheeka's physical appearance.

"I'm…I'm twelve."

"Twelve? Twelve? Oh, hell no! I'm calling the police! Twelve?"

"No! Wait, please." Sheeka explains, "They will kill me and my family!"

"Who? Who's going to hurt you and your family?"

"The tall guy out there with the black tee shirt and ripped jeans. His name is Dom."

"Okay, okay. Let me think," as he paces the floor back and forth. "I'm going to get you out of here." He looks at the clock and notices he still has thirty minutes left for his session. They sit quietly thinking of a plan when Sheeka humbly asks him, "Can I please call my mom?" "Sure," he turns and gives her his phone.

Sheeka takes the phone and quickly called her mom to tell her that she is in Atlanta, but she was not sure of her exact location. The guy helping her took the phone and gave her mom the location then ended the call. He tells Sheeka, "I'm going to call your mom back when I leave here. I'm going to get you out of here, I promise. Just keep working as usual. You have to act like nothing happened."

"I'm scared they're going to kill me!"

"Trust me! I'm going to help you, but you gotta be cool." They wait out the remaining 20 minutes of his session. He looks back at her and says, "Stay strong and positive until your rescue." He and his friends leave the parlor. Trying to act normal, he says to his friends, "Hey. Let's go around the corner." When they got to the parking lot, he revealed everything about Sheeka to his friends.

One of the friends responded, "Seriously, bro? Go to the police and tell them so they can go get her." The guy said, "I have to call her mom back." Another friend said, "I seen this on TV before. It's called human or sex trafficking. Crazy…." The guy that was with Sheeka suggested, "Listen, we have to do something. We have to help, she's only 12 years old! Man, my little sister is twelve!! Get the fuck out of here!"

In Newark, Reverend Briggs had another prayer vigil for the girls. Praying for their release from their captors and that God would soften their hearts. Warfare prayer is set for tonight's service at seven p.m., thanking God for the return of Nia.

As soon as Vivian ended the call with Sheeka, she called Detective Malone to give him the information she had just received. He contacted a detective in Atlanta and the detectives were on their way. Vivian let out a sudden and long horrifying scream! All at once her thoughts caught up to her. The thought of her baby prostituting was more than she could handle. She grieved as someone who had lost their child would have grieved.

Kat and Boots heard her scream. Kat made it to her apartment first and ran in since Vivian's door stays open. She found Vivian curled up on the floor crying uncontrollably. Kat ran over to her, "Vivian, what's going on? Are you okay? What happened?" Vivian can only get out "Sheeka!" Boots then runs in and picks Vivian up off the floor. Kat gets a wet paper towel and wipes her face.

Boots asked, 'What's wrong Viv? What is it?" She managed to pull herself together enough to answer, "Sheeka called me! She's working in a massage parlor in Atlanta! My baby..." Kat interrupts, "Oh shit!" Boots and Vivian both look at her, that was not the response they were looking for. Realizing her odd reaction, Kat asked, "So did you call the police?" Vivian responded, "Yes, they're on their way." Kat leaves the apartment unexpectedly and runs downstairs to her apartment. With deep suspicion, Boots waited until he heard her door close, then he told Vivian he'd be right back and ran to the basement. Kat quickly makes a phone call and screams to the person on the other end, "What the hell is going on, stupid?! The girl in Atlanta has contacted her mother!"

Boots is now putting the pieces together. He believes Kat is behind it all. He ran back to Vivian's apartment to console Vivian before Kat got back. He gave her a glass of water and the police arrive. Boots stays with Vivian, but notices that Kat never came back. When he looked out the kitchen window, he saw Kat get into her car and pull off in a hurry.

At the same time, in Atlanta, multiple police cars surround the front and rear of the Magic Hands Massage Parlor. Everyone inside was apprehended. Sheeka was taken down to the station but not before she collapsed of starvation in the arms of an officer. Dom resisted arrest and was taken to the hospital for his injuries where he laid handcuffed to the bed. Men and women were also rescued from the nail salon by police officers, Sheeka had informed them that they were being used for forced labor. Relief had overtaken Sheeka as the officers placed a blanket around her and sat her in a police car while they got her something to eat.

Meanwhile, Boots returned to the basement and went to the door that lead to Kat's apartment. He always knew it was there but had never been given a reason to open it before. Until now. Not for a second does he question his old-time skills he learned on the streets. He picked the lock with ease and stepped into her living room. He goes into her bedroom to start searching. He wasn't sure what he was looking for but there had to be something. He enters her closet and finds a strong box. He grabs it and leaves without any evidence of his entry. He picks the box open and pulled out papers onto the makeshift folding table; coming across her marriage certificate with pictures of her wedding two years ago. 'Married? Two years ago?' He thought. The bottom of the photo was dated and engraved May 3, 2015. Eric Morales and Kat were married on Isla Verde beach in Puerto Rico.

Then, he finds an article from a newspaper with bold headlines stating, *"CONVICTION OVERTURNED, all witnesses were mysteriously killed."* 'OH SHIT! It's Kat's husband, Eric Morales!' Boots is nervously entertaining thoughts in his mind. He put the file back in the strong box and placed it back in her apartment. He goes back to the basement, sitting in the dark in shock!

Chapter 11

Quianna Meets Her Client

Back in San Fernando, Quianna still wasn't sure how Quinn felt after her advancements. After that day, he never mentioned it again, so she decides to make a plan to escape. She begins to pray, 'Lord, I know I haven't been the best and my disobedience has gotten me into a lot of trouble. I'm scared and I need you. Help Me! You said if I called on you, you would help me. Keep Nia and Sheeka safe. God get Rico, especially because he tricked me. Get those other guys too and hurt them bad for taking us. You said you would protect us, in Jesus Name.'

Quinn comes back all business like and extremely focused. Nothing can shake him. He takes Quianna to the vineyards to meet with her client. There is silence in the car and it's awkward as hell. Neither of them said a word the whole ride. Quinn tells her he will be back to pick her up in the morning unless she is requested to stay another day. They arrive at the massive estate with high-tech surveillance cameras, a wrought iron security gate and winding driveway. He gives Quianna a dose of ecstasy before pulling up to the gate. She looks at him but finds it hard to read his mood. Then she turns her attention to the property, it's apparent that this client is filthy rich.

The gate opens up and the town car enters. Quinn drives in and as he approaches the pool house, the housekeeper comes to greet him. He opens the door for Quianna, retrieves her overnight bag, and gives it to the housekeeper. Saying nothing, he got back in the car and then exited the property. Quianna was sure she had blown it with him. She starts feeling the drugs kicking in and loosens up. She was then led to a room where her client was waiting. They were introduced and the housekeeper left.

Quianna engaged in small-talk and complimented him on his gorgeous estate. She asked him for a tour, but her body was doing something else. The pill was working now, and Mr. "Winery" wanted to retire in the pool room. He grabbed a bottle of Romanée-Conte Grand Cru and placed it in the chiller, then sat two long stemmed wine glasses on the table and began to entertain "Ms. Quianna" as he called her. He fed her stuffed mushrooms and bacon wrapped shrimp on a skewer, then told her what was expected of her. By now, the pill was in full effect. She had been doing this now for three months, so she knew how to perform. She began to dance and even though there was no music playing, for some reason they vibed well together. She felt comfortable around him, considering it was her first time meeting him. She asked him to put something on that she could groove to, he watches her closely as her body moves with the music. She made him feel like he was twenty again. He grabs her hand, and they move to the beat of the music. As he closes his eyes and pulls her in close, his hands rest on her waist. The fragrance of her hair reminded him of a former love. He began to make up words to the beat of the song, Quianna laughed to herself as she listened.

Back in New York, Eric Morales lands at the JFK Airport and makes it to his suite at the Crown Plaza Hotel. Aponte had stayed behind to oversee operations back home, but the rest of his entourage came with him. Four well-dressed men with suits, ties, and pitch-black Ray-Ban sunglasses. They looked intimidating and were definitely packing. The construction crew who would handle the renovations at the "Bricks" was there as well. They all went to Eric Morales' hotel for a quick meeting with the management company director. They had dinner and drinks and went over the plans for the building renovations and hotel accommodations for the tenants and the construction crew. The management director leaves, and their meeting begins.

Eric Morales directs his attention toward the construction crew, "No quiero que hablen con mi mujer. No quiero que ni siquiera la miren." (I don't want you talking to my woman, don't even acknowledge her). The crew shook their heads nervously in agreement to his wishes and they continued with the renovation plans. The top apartment would be done first. There will be a two -week displacement. The apartment overhaul will get new floors, painted walls, new bathroom vanities, new ceiling fans and countertops.

He informed them that more guys would be coming in for the renovations. "I want everything done in two weeks. The whole project should take four months. No more. My business isn't your business. Go to the hotel in Newark and remember, don't talk to my wife or talk about her to anyone." The construction crew nodded their heads, wrapped up the plans and left.

Morales was furious when he got the news about his girls and the possible exposure of the organization.

"You morons! I pay you to do a job and you can't even accomplish that?! Who's this Rico character?"

"Aponte's cousin, sir. Aponte had just brought him on," replied one of his men.

"Well, this is his first and last time creating a problem. I'm a professional! I've been in this business a very long time. I want this boy handled! He's done enough! Take him out NOW!"

The word is given to take Rico out.

As soon as Quinn got the order, he called Rico to give him a heads up. They're close and practically grew up together. As they talked, Quinn wasn't sure if he should keep the hit to himself or tell the others, but it's Eric Morales we're talking about. He would take out his own brother with no thought, almost as easy as picking his teeth. He thinks to himself, 'It's either me or Rico - sorry bro.'

Quinn and Rico are on the phone, and without holding it much longer; he interrupts Rico and blurts out, "Man, Eric put a hit out on you! They're coming to kill you - get out of there!" He hangs up as soon as he said it. Rico was shocked, replaying Quinn's words in his head. He was shaken and left the blue house immediately right after he got all the money out of the safe that was built into the floor. He caught a taxi and left before Eric Morales' men could take the three-hour ride to Albany, NY. He heads to the train station not sure where he's going but knowing he couldn't stay there.

Sheeka Calls Home

Sheeka tells the FBI everything she knows but starts shaking and sweating. She needed her fix and couldn't concentrate. She gets agitated and confused over the line of questioning, one after another after another. Suddenly, she screams, "I'm the damn victim here! You're questioning me like I'm the bad guy!" She didn't know she was addicted to heroin, she just felt uptight and on edge. Sheeka called her mom Vivian on the phone.

Sheeka yells, "MOM!" Vivian, in both relief and angst, answered "Oh my God! Sheeka? Are you alright?"

"Come get me the hell out of here!" As she listened to her voice, Vivian realized this wasn't the same twelve-year old that had left her months ago! "Where are you, sweetie?"

"Atlanta. At the police station. Mom, please, come get me! PLEASE!"

"Baby, I don't have any money to come get you. Let me speak to the police officer, maybe they can bring you home." Sheeka goes off, "What kind of shit is this? Someone kidnaps me, your daughter, and you can't even come get my ass! Maybe you should get up off your ass and get a job, so you'll have some damn money! What the fuck! Mom, you can't even come get me?" Vivian is hurt and shocked by her response. "Sheeka, baby, what's wrong with you? Why are you talking like that?"

"What's wrong with me? What's wrong with me?! You're a poor excuse for a mother! That's what's wrong with me!"

Realizing her increased agitation and disrespect, an officer took the phone out of her hand. Special Agent Daniels intervenes and says, "Ma'am, I'm Special Agent Daniels, I'm sorry, your daughter has been through a lot. We must be sensitive to the trauma she has endured. She was rescued from a massage parlor here in Atlanta which is currently under investigation. Are you able to come pick up your daughter?"

Vivian is crying, "What's wrong with her?"

"I'm so sorry. It seems she's on some type of drug. We're not quite sure what yet, but we will find all of this out. We believe this is how she was controlled, and she's going to have a long road to recovery. I apologize."

Vivian pleaded, "I can't afford to come get her. Is there any way? Can you send her to me?"

"Yes ma'am. Of course. We will make arrangements to get her home. It might take a couple of days, but we will get her home to you."

"Thank you so much Agent Daniels. Thank you for saving my girl. Thank you!"

Chapter 12

Rico Needs Help

Back in Jersey, Shae is falling for Larry again. They've been spending quite a bit of time together. He's keeping her close with his lies and his seductive ways. Her face has healed by now and so had her heart. He's staying with her at the hotel while her apartment is being renovated and Shae comes home only to grab clothes or bills. Bett is watching after Monster, not sure if her mom lost her mind after Larry beat her ass. Frustrated with Shae, Bett says, "Are you crazy, mom? Don't you see what he's doing? He's using you, trying to manipulate you. Your buggin', this is the same man who left you for dead! He'll probably do it again!"

"Mind your damn business, Bett! This is my life and you're my child; I'm the mom! So stay in your place!"

"Mom? You don't even care about your kids!"

"You're a liar! Don't you dare say that! My kids are my life!"

"Larry and his cousins came to fight Blue. They were looking to kill him! Why would you stay with him? Why mom?" Shae looked at her like she was crazy and asked, "What? Wait! What happened?" Bett filled her in, "Blue beat Larry up for putting his hands on you, mom. Larry came after Blue with his cousins. That's why Blue had to relocate to another club, but you wouldn't know that cause he's playing you for a fool!"

"I didn't know, I must have been in the hospital."

"Your kids are your life right? What are you going to do now mom? Now that you do know?'

"I'm going to confront Larry!"

"What? Why…so he can beat you down again? No! Just stay here, don't go back. Save yourself mom! Come on…wake up!"

"I'm going to get my stuff. I'll be right back." Bett yells, "No, Mom! Don't go! Let me go with you!" Shae insisted, "No, I can handle this. I'll be right back!" And she stormed out the door.

At the bodega, Mr. Tony gets a call from Rico. "Tio?"

"Rico? Where are you boy?"

"I need your help! They have a hit out on me!"

"Nephew, you caused trouble to this family. I tried to help you!"

"Uncle, please. They are going to kill me…please!"

"Rico, listen to me. Tell me the truth. Did you have anything to do with those girls being kidnapped?"

Rico hesitated for about five seconds and lies, "No, I didn't. I swear. You have to believe me. I need you!"

"Call your mother Rico! You have to tell me and your mother the whole truth if you want me to help you." Rico gets frustrated and says, "Never mind! I knew I shouldn't have called you," slamming the phone down.

A while back, Eric Morales had gotten a tip that Quinn might be an undercover cop who had turned into a trafficker. He finally received confirmation that he was a police officer in the Narcotics Special Investigation Unit sent out to bust drug lords. While undercover he got hooked on coke. He saw how money was being made so he double dipped and would give the police information while trafficking on the side. He was bringing more money in with trafficking than he was being on the force. Quinn went dark for three years. Eric

Morales hired him, unaware that he was former law enforcement.

The "Bricks" Remodeling

Right before the remodeling started, Tootie left out the apartment with her car full of her belongings. The workers begin to flirt with her. "Hey beautiful, I'm going to make your place extra special!" Tootie is flattered and loved the attention. "What is your name pretty lady?" Tootie fired back, "What's yours?" "Sosa, and this is Toño," pointing to the other worker. "Nice to meet you!" Tootie asked, "What exactly will you be doing and how long will it take?"

"A week or a week and a half," the man replied in his broken English. Tootie never mentions anything about her missing daughter. She wanted to get back to her place in case Quianna arrived. She stops in her tracks, "By the way, I'm Tootie."

She gets into her car and Sosa runs down the brownstone steps to ask, "So you're going to be at the Suites?"

"Yes. I am. How did you know?"

"We are staying there too. Maybe we can get something to eat sometime?" '

"We'll see." She smiled, but the smile faded quickly as she began to feel guilty for thinking about enjoying herself when her daughter is missing. Sadness fell on her as she left the last place her and her daughter shared for fourteen years. She prayed silently, 'Lord, send me my baby back! I've made a huge mistake. What did I do? Lord, what did I do? I'm sorry! I miss her. Forgive me, forgive me Lord!'

Eric's men reached Albany, but when they arrived at the blue house there was no Rico in sight. They waited until morning for Rico to come. But Rico never showed, and he wasn't answering his phone. They called Mr. Morales to give him the update and unfortunate news of Rico's disappearance. Someone had obviously tipped him off or he would have answered his phone by now, waiting for instruction. There is a leak in the camp and Mr. Morales was livid.

Construction Day

Construction has started at the "Bricks". Four workers begin the remodeling work. Two men are in Shae's apartment and two are in Tootie's. Two more guys arrived shortly after to join the project overhaul. Boots asked one of the workers if they were hiring so they took him to the guy in charge, the foreman. The foreman could use the extra help, so after much thought, he tells Boots, "I'll hire you for seventy dollars a day. You have to run the trash and debris to the dumpster." Not only did Boots need the money, but he also needed information from the guys. So, Boots decided to make some conversation, "Hey, so who owns Morales & Company? Do you guys do much work here?" He's asking questions while removing the sheet rock that was just ripped from the walls. Toño replied, "No, man. We just came to do this job." So, Boots tells them, "I'm good friends with Kat Morales. It's all good. She told me everything. That's how I knew you were coming. You don't have to hide anything with me. I know it all!" Toño and Sosa look at each other reluctantly.

Boots, realizing he might have given too much too quick, backtracks, "Oh…but don't tell her that I told you. She'd be really upset. No one else should know." They believed him and are more comfortable and open when they talk to him. In conversation, he gets confirmation about the verdict overturning, witnesses mysteriously disappearing until there was no one to testify against him. To keep gaining their trust, he tells them, "The police are thick around here so carry your I.D."

"Why? What's going on around here? Is this a drug area?"

"No, three little girls went missing from this building. Two of them were already found. But there's still one out there."

Toño asked, "found where?" Boots confirms, "New York & the other in Atlanta." Toño exclaimed, "Wow! Really," as he glances at Sosa and mutters, "Bizzi." Sosa shook his head yes. He then asked Boots, "Have they heard anything about the last girl?"

"No."

Toño puts his tools on the table. Sosa and Toño are working on Tootie's apartment now. Sosa asked Boots, "So you know Bizzi?"

"Bizzi? Who's that?"

Toño answered, "Eric Morales."

"Oh. I just know Kat. She's been living here for years. We're good friends." Sosa continued to test Boots and see how much he really knows, "So, how long they been married?" Boots answers, "Oh…2 years. Yeah, they got married on Isla Verde Beach, Kat told me all about it. She confides in me. Who am I going to tell? Hell, I live in the alley!" They all laughed. Then, Boots asked,

"Does he own any more properties around here?" Sosa answered, "Yeah, and he's here to buy 5 more brown stones." Boots acts impressed and says, "Damn, he must be living nice."

Toño confirmed, "Yeah. He's doing well." Boots replied, "So where's the other properties?"

"He has one near here. Chan the Karate guy is the manager."

"The karate teacher who teaches Quianna?"

"Quianna? Who's that?"

"Oh! The lady's daughter who lives in this apartment. She's the last one missing. She was kidnapped."

Sosa interjects, "The lady who lives here? That girl is her daughter? I mean, she didn't seem too upset. She didn't even mention it." Boots tells them, "It's been months now. She's dealing with it in her own way." He brings down some sheet rock and sees Kat going into her apartment as he goes to the dumpster.

"Hey Kat! How are you doing today?"

"I'm okay. I'm in a rush, I can't talk right now. I have to run in and out." Boots was glad she was leaving, now she can't talk to Sosa and Toño. "Okay. Talk to you later." Running up the steps, she sees Jean in the window and nods her head without really speaking. Kat leaves out and gets into her car. She waved at Mr. Willie sitting on the bench in front of his cleaners.

Meanwhile, Rico has no other options. He's running out of money and has no where to go. So, he calls his uncle again. Tony answered the phone, "Tony's Bodega." Rico speaks urgently into the phone, "Tio, I need you to help me. They are going to kill me. Come get me Tio please!" Tony could hear the desperation in his voice, but said, "No, you lied to me! Tell me the truth and I'll help you!"

"You put strangers before me?" and hung up on his uncle a second time. Mr. Tony wrote down the number from his caller ID.

The Meridian Suites

Kat drove over to the hotel to check on Shae and her accommodations. She needed to make sure Shae was satisfied with her new place for the next two weeks, so she could give a report to her husband. Kat entered the slick and modernly designed front lobby of the Meridian Suites Hotel. She bypasses the front desk and heads straight for Shae's room on the first floor. As she turns the corner and reaches Shae's door, Larry comes out of the stairwell with a bucket of ice. They both stop. "What the hell you doin' here? You're not coming to see Shae! Anyway, she's not here, now leave!"

"Leave? Me, leave? If anybody will be leaving, it's going to be you! Don't make me call my boys! Who do you think you are?"

Their voices are getting louder and they are causing a disturbance in the hallway. The front desk clerk hears the commotion and goes to the end of the corridor. "Hello? Is everything okay down there. Do you need me to call security?" They both look back and lower their voices. Kat answers, "No, we're fine!" She was not trying to bring any attention to them or, especially, herself. They head for the stairwell where the door shuts. Kat continued, "You need to leave Shae alone, you low-life thug!"

"Your mouth is so slick! Bitch, why don't you kick my ass yourself? Remember you told me, you ain't Shae? Then, jump bitch! Jump!" Kat lunges forward but she doesn't hit him. He punches her in the face, and she falls to the floor, dazed. She begins to lose consciousness. But when she gets herself up, she regains her composure and swings at him. Larry lost it! He was used to women staying down, but Kat wasn't going down without a fight! He punched her repeatedly in the face and body leaving her completely unconscious this time. He stuffed her limp body under the stairwell and took her purse and broken cell phone.

This time Larry had gone too far, and he knew it. He headed to Shae's room to shower and change his clothes because Kat's blood was all over him. His hand wouldn't stop bleeding. He wrapped a hand towel around it, tightly. Shae wasn't back yet from her breakfast date with Bett and Monster who was staying with her sister. As he gets dressed, he tries to calm down. He wasn't remorseful about what happened, but he was aware of exactly what he had done. His phone rings, it was Rico on the other end.

"Yo man, I need you," a nervous tremor resounded in Rico's voice. Larry asked him, "What's wrong dog?"

"I'm in some trouble. Someone is after me. Can you come get me now?"

"Where are you?"

"I'm at Penn Station. Call me when you get here. I'll come out."

"Aight. I'll be there in about 20 minutes."

Back at the hotel, Eric Morales wanted to know about the undercover cop that went bad. He needed to make sure he wasn't working from the inside. He asked Paco his bodyguard, "Where's my wife? She should have been here by now. Call her!" Paco calls as instructed, but no answer. Mr. Morales tells him to try again in 10 minutes.

After Larry hung up with Rico, he took the hand towel off and laid it on the bathroom counter, he grabbed his shades, Kat's phone, and left. He throws Kat's phone in a Burger King bag and tossed it in the dumpster on his way out and heads for Penn Station. He calls Rico and instructs him to come out through the front entrance.

"Yo man! You look scared as hell. Are you okay?" Larry half-jokingly wondered what Rico had gotten himself into. "Nah. This dude is after me. He put out a hit on me, man. He's nothing to play with! Hey. What's wrong with your hand? You are bleeding and shit!"

"Yeah, it's nothing. I had to handle something, that's all."

"What…you beat Shae up again?" Rico snarked as he spoke.

"No…I beat the shit out of that bitch Kat!"

Rico's expression completely changed, and he was terrified, "What? Kat, Kat? Kat from the Bricks? The one on the bottom floor with the blonde dreads? That Kat?"

"Yeah, her ass won't get smart with me no more!"

"Oh Shit!" He realized Larry had made a grave mistake, but he didn't even know it. "No!! Man, noooooooooooo!" Larry said, "What?"

"What? Man, that's Eric Morales' wife! You fucked up! You messed with the wrong one, bro! OH MY GOD! He's going to kill you! He's like Scarface, only worse! This man is notorious for killing people! He has a hit out on me! He killed all the witnesses for his drug trial. What did you do? We gotta leave now! Where's his wife? Does she know who you are?"

"It doesn't matter, she won't be talking for a while! And I ain't scared of no Eric Morales." "Well, you should be…damn! Where is she, Larry?" Larry bragging, "She can't even talk! I knocked her ass out! We're fine."

"She's got to wake up at some point. We have to leave and head south. Do you have any money?"

"Are you nuts? I can't go on the run! I have to go to work tonight!"

"Bro…you are not listening! Don't you get it? You'll be dead by then!"

"Damn, it's like that?" Now Rico got Larry's attention. "YES! Now drive!" Larry drove to his place and grabbed some clothes, stuffed it in a black backpack and they headed for NJ Turnpike South.

Chapter 13

Boots Gets Suspicious

Boots was still cleaning Tootie's apartment when he sees the Karate teacher pull up and meet Jean at the apartment entrance. Through the window, he can see Chan give Jean an envelope. She opened it and rolled her fingers through a stack of money, then she puts it back in the envelope. They exchange a few more words, then she goes in the building and he leaves. Boots watched all this take place and noticed Chan come back from his car talk to Tootie as she pulled up in front of the building. Whatever he said to her made her cry hysterically. He pointed to Jean's apartment, then left. Boots ran down to her car to console her. He asked, "Tootie, are you okay?" "Yeah Boots, I'm fine. Just thinking about my baby." Mr. Willie comes out to check out the scene, then Tootie pulls off.

Mr. Willie yelled over to Boots, "You see that?"

"I did," Boots yelled back, crossing the street. Jean was looking at both of them from her window, but she couldn't make out what they were saying.

"Now why did he give Jean all that money? She's on welfare."

"Some strange shit is happening around here, Willie!" Toño came out and saw Boots across the street talking to Mr. Willie. "Hey! Are you quitting on me?" Boots turned from his conversation, "No, here I come! I'm coming!" He heads back across the street to the 'Bricks'.

A fiend named Erika comes staggering onto the stoop and starts yelling out names while scratching, "Kat...Ricky! Ronnie! Where the fuck are you? Come the hell out here!" She's gets louder, bringing attention to the area.

While all this was going down, two undercover cops were parked by the church; watching, waiting, and taking notes. They were now fully aware that Kat and her boys were selling drugs out of their building. Jean looked down from her window and tells the fiend to shut up! She tells her that Kat isn't there and to get away from the building. The fiend walks around the corner near the church and the cops pay her off. Mr. Willie is watching everything as it's happening, noticing Jean was never so verbal before. Jean left her window to call Kat on her phone, but it just rings.

At the bodega, Mr. Tony was thinking long and hard about helping his nephew. Family is always first to him. He can't get Rico's voice and words out of his head. 'You pick them over me.' In Puerto Rico, his sister is worried sick about her boy. She hadn't heard from him since he left to work for her brother in New Jersey.

Back at Tootie's apartment, Boots is listening to Toño and Sosa speaking Spanish. He understands their conversation because he learned the language in school. They are speaking pretty intensely. Boots heard Toño say, "Bizzi is going kill those guys for letting those girls get away. Why did they take the girls to his apartment? That was why he was so mad when we left him." "I don't know. The lady here didn't seem too upset that they took her daughter, though." Toño replied, "Not at all. It can't be her daughter. Maybe that man was wrong."

Boots entered the apartment. Sosa asked Boots in English, "Hey man, you say the lady here, her daughter is missing?" "Yes." They walk into the living room and Boots shows him a box with pictures frames, then picks it up. "The first picture is with Quianna and Tootie." Boots begins to cry and walks out the room. Toño followed him and pat his back as if he was feeling Boots' pain. He then says in Spanish, "This is some bullshit." Boots keeps his head down so he could hear more. Sosa commented back in Spanish, "Maybe he's mad because the police are on them now and his wife can't do her thing." Boots lifts his head, drying his eyes and walks to the kitchen; hoping they will continue talking freely.

Eric Morales

It's now 8:00 p.m. and Eric Morales still can't reach his wife. He hasn't heard from her all day which is not like her. The last time they talked was 8:30 that morning. He called her phone again and it went straight to voicemail. He sent his guys to check for his wife and tells them, "Don't come back here without an answer! Find my wife!" He's getting nervous and his guys had never seen this side of him before.

Jean called Kat's phone once again. This was her 5th time calling, and it's still going to voicemail. She calls the phone number she dreads calling, which was given to her only for extreme emergencies. Jean called Eric Morales. "He-hello…Mr. Morales, this is Jean from the Bricks. I'm trying to reach Kat and it's very important that I speak with her."

Mr. Morales replied, "I can't reach her either. Where's my wife?!" He listened to what she had to say but tells her by any means necessary to find her! He slammed the phone down, his worry increasing now that Jean called.

Shae comes back to the hotel, after not having heard from Larry all day. He wasn't returning any of her calls. When she stepped inside the room, she saw Larry wasn't there, but found blood droplets on the floor and on the counter. She starts to worry and calling him again. Still no answer.

Her phone rings and she jumps to answer, hoping it was Larry calling back. But it was Rico. Rico says, "Shae, I'm calling for Larry. He had to take an unexpected trip out of town for a family emergency. He said he will call you when he gets there," and he ended the call immediately. Shae was puzzled, she never got to ask if Larry was okay or about the blood in the bathroom. And she never heard him talk about his family before.

The Karate teacher showed up to the "Bricks" and Boots came out from the alley. Boots sees him and says, "What's up man?" Chan replied, "Hey. Is Tootie here?"

"No, I haven't seen her today. Do you want me to relay a message when I see her? I can, no problem. Man, I'm sure you're missing Quianna, huh?"

"Yes, I am. It's terrible, huh?" Before Boots can go on, Sosa comes out and greets Chan. "Hey, Chan." Chan hesitated but raises his hand slowly. Boots looked over at Chan and asked, "You know him?" Chan looking uncomfortable and tells him, "Uh. Tell Tootie, I'll be back." He got back in his car and sped off. Sosa answered Boots' question, "Yeah, he's one of the apartments managers." Boots is starting to put things together but is curious why Chan wanted to see Tootie. Jean walks in on the last part of the conversation, so she wasn't sure what she heard. The guys finished for the day right around 8:30 pm. Boots hollered over to Jean, "Hey Jean!"

"Hey Boots, you can understand those guys?"

"A little, just a little," changing the subject, "Have you seen Tootie? Quianna's Karate teacher is looking for her."

"I don't know, but I think he likes her," Jean smirked.

"What? That's fucked up. You're telling me her daughter is missing, so he takes the opportunity to try to holler at her? I hope you're wrong."

"Ugh, okay. Have you seen Kat?"

"She left this morning early, I saw her when she left. Don't know where she was headed."

"I haven't been able to reach her all day." She returned to her apartment.

Paco and the other bodyguard went to the apartment building to look for Kat. They knocked on the door but there was no answer. They continue knocking for at least 3 more minutes and then use their key to get in. Te'nah saw them go into Kat's apartment. She ran back up the stairs and called the police.

911 operator, "911...what's your emergency?"

Te'nah tells the operator, "There's a break-in in my apartment building! Hurry!"

"Okay, stay calm. What's the address?" Te'nah gives her the address. The operator probed for more information, "Okay, what's your name?" Te'nah gives her name and the operator asked further, "Who's apartment is it? Are they home?" Te'nah answered, "It's Ms. Kat and no, I don't think she's home. They just went to her apartment; 2 big men in black suits, one Hispanic, and one white. I don't know how they got in!"

"Okay. We're sending someone now. Stay away, go in your apartment. They're on the way!" The 911 dispatcher radios police officers with the location and, since there were already officers in the vicinity because of the recent events, it wasn't long before police sirens were blazing. They surround the building. When they approach Ms. Kat's apartment, they saw the door was opened slightly. They went in, apprehended the two men, and took them into custody for breaking and entering.

Three hours had passed by and Mr. Morales hadn't heard from his guys. He called the construction worker, Sosa, and asked him to go to the apartment and see if his men had found his wife.

Thirty minutes pass by, still no news.

Jean called Mr. Morales, "Hi, um, Mr. Morales; it's Jean again, I haven't heard from Kat but there were some men in her apartment, and they got arrested for breaking and entering."

"Damn! I'm firing everyone, they're all imbeciles. Where would my wife go, you don't think she got locked up do you?"

"Oh...I never thought of that. Let me call the police and the local hospital, I'll call you back!"

At Meridian Suites, the stairway door slammed loudly. A little girl was going up the stairs and dropped her ball and it rolled to the bottom of the staircase. Her mother went to retrieve it for her. When they reached the bottom of the stairway, they were startled to see a female in a fetal position under the stairwell. The woman grabbed her daughter, ran through the door, screaming down the hall past Shae's room as she headed for the front desk.

Shae was startled and came out of her door, but no one was there. The Hotel Manager and Hotel Security ran down the hall towards the staircase to check out the situation.

The manager was shaking, "She…she looks dead!"

Security called 911 and blocked off the second floor and the ground floor stairway entrances while they wait for the ambulance to arrive.

Shae is watching everything from her hotel room door but was told to stay inside her room, the other guests on her floor were given the same instruction. Kat is carried out and into the ambulance. Shae tried to get a good view, but never got to see who the person was in the emergency vehicle.

Meanwhile, Jean called the Newark Police Department, hoping she can get something on Kat's location. But there's no one there by that name. Then she calls the hospital and Kat was not there either. So she calls Mr. Morales back with the unfortunate news.

Mr. Morales answered, "Did you hear anything, yet?"

"No. I'm sorry, she's not at the hospital or jail."

"Oh my God, where is my wife?! Why can't anyone find her?"

Sosa went back to the "Bricks' and he sees Boots standing just outside of the building's entrance. Sosa asked Boots "Hey, man. Why are the police here?"

"Some guys got arrested for breaking into an apartment," Boots answered as he pointed to Kat's apartment.

"Oh wow. Hey, have you seen Ms. Kat?"

"Not all day. You know, you're the second person looking for her. Maybe she's with her husband."

"No, he's the one looking for her. If you see her call me immediately!" He gave Boots his number, and Boots inquired, "Those guys who got arrested were probably after her? They broke into her apartment." "I don't know. I will have to find out." Sosa wasn't about to give up information to Boots, his orders are coming from Bizzi, and he's not going to cross him over a bum in the alley.

At the hospital where Tootie works, Kat arrived with severe head trauma, broken ribs, a bruised liver, and some missing front teeth. Her face is unrecognizable, her eyes are shut, and face swollen. She was prepped for emergency surgery to relieve the pressure from her brain. Tootie could see a lady being rushed into the emergency room on the stretcher but she had no idea it was Kat. She was listed as an unidentified person and had no I.D. or purse. And it didn't help that she was in a coma. Sosa called Mr. Morales to tell him that his men were arrested, but he already knew that because Jean had informed him. Eric Morales told Sosa to book plane tickets for the other two guys coming from Puerto Rico. Sosa said he was not sure if he could handle that so Mr. Morales calls Jean. Jean answered on the first ring. "Jean, I need you to do some work for me. I will take care of you. Don't worry." Jean replied, "Okay." After all, who says no to Eric Morales? "Good. I'm sending a car for you now. Be ready." and he hung up.

Chapter 14

Jean meets Mr. Morales

A car service arrived to pick Jean up and, an hour later, she was at Eric Morales' suite at the Crown Plaza. His bodyguard opened the door and Jean walked in slowly, a little nervous to meet Mr. Morales. He was engaged in a conversation that seemed very important. She made sure to stay extra quiet so as to not interrupt. He finally turned around, saw Jean, and ended his call. Jean looked at him anxiously, "Hello, Mr. Morales."

"You can call me Bizzi, pretty lady." He took her hand and spun her around, checking her out from head to toe, like he normally does with the women he meets. Mr. Morales lets go of Jean's hand and walks over to his bar, "I'm going crazy over here. I want my wife and I need to get my guys back!"

"Hmm...I can help you. Give me the names of your guys. Do you have someone in Newark who can go to the bail bondsman once they get bail?"

"The workers can go take care of that. I'd rather pay cash."

"Um, Mr. Morales, if the bail is high, I don't recommend cash. You'll be bringing attention to yourself or your guys. It's uncommon."

"Yes, I didn't think of that. You handle it and I'll take care of the payment." Jean calls the police station and gets the bail information. She found out Paco has a murder charge, so he won't be getting out until the authorities extradite him back to Puerto Rico. The other guy has a gun charge in Puerto Rico. He was out on bail there so he will also be extradited to Puerto Rico. Mr. Morales now had a missing wife and two bodyguards in jail, so he only had 2 guards, his driver and his construction workers. So far, his trip to the U.S. had not gone very well.

Jean booked two tickets from Puerto Rico to the New York for two more of Mr. Morales' goons. There were still two guys who were after Rico, but they hadn't found him yet. Mr. Morales decided to call them back, given his circumstances. He needed to let off some steam, so he grabbed a bottle of E&J Vanilla Brandy and pours some in his glass. He offered Jean a drink and she accepts. After he gives her the glass, he throws $300 on the table for her help. Sighing with relief that some of his business is being taken care of and his guys would be joining him in a couple of hours, he pulled out a Cuban cigar, relaxed, and engaged in conversation with Jean. An hour passed and half the bottle was already gone. Jean felt a little woozy and asked if she could use the bathroom. As she gets up to walk away, Mr. Morales turned his head and was checking her out. The sounds of Latin music was playing, the lights were dim, bamboo musk candles were burning; the atmosphere was quite relaxing which was always Mr. Morales' preference.

She returned from the bathroom and sat back on the couch. They continued talking when he asks her if she'd like to take on more responsibility. He tells her he could use her near him in his operation while he's in the states. Jean was eager to get into the business, but more flattered that Mr. Morales asked her himself. So she quickly answered, "Yes! Absolutely…. This isn't going to be a problem for Kat, though, is it?" Morales looked at her sternly and said, "No. Not at all, I'll take care of her! She has no say in whatever I do!" He poured the last of the bottle in his glass as his apple cigar filled the air. Then, he walked around the counter to grab another bottle of E&J. Jean's eyes were fixed on his strong masculine physique. Mr. Morales is very attractive, he was well-groomed, and his cologne was nothing like she'd ever smelled before. From the corner of his eye, he could tell she was admiring him.

When he sat back down, he made sure to position himself closer to her and his knee touched hers. He gazed into her eyes and tells her how beautiful they are. Jean blushed at the compliment and thanked him. The conversation suddenly stops, and he leans in to kiss her, but she begins to back away unsure of what was about to take place. He placed his drink on the shelf behind the couch, grabbed her neck, and pulled her in close. Then, he gently kisses her lips. Jean closed her eyes, wanting to stop but enjoying it all at once, she begins to kiss him back, then she kisses his neck. Getting into the heat of the moment, she ran her nails down his spine which drives him crazy. He laid her back on the couch and starts panting as he is already aroused. Jean grabbed the back of his head, kissing him passionately. Morales slowly grabs the bottom of her shirt to remove it over her head. Just as he takes her shirt off, she knocked over his drink with her hand and it spills all over him and the couch. He jumped up and walked to the bar to dry himself off and refresh his glass. Jean put her shirt back on and ties her dreads up, realizing what almost happened. "Eric, umm Bizzi, I don't think this is right. Kat has been my friend for years. We really shouldn't...." Eric became agitated and threw his glass across the room and it shattered on the wall. Jean jumped unexpectedly. "You don't want to do that shit with me. I don't play games!" He poured another drink into a new glass and slammed it on the counter.

"I just didn't want to mess up my friendship with Kat. I don't think…."

"You already did! You're no friend of hers. Your mine now! Now, let's try this again." Walking towards Jean; he undid his pants, grabbed himself and grabbed her by the arm. Jean resisted but Mr. Morales smacked her to the floor. Her mouth immediately started to bleed as she turned to watch him standing over her. "Don't do that shit again. Do not resist me, Chiquita. You do what I tell you. Understand?"

Jean started crying from both pain and embarrassment, "Please! I want to leave!" He grabbed her by her dreads and pulled her back to the couch.

"I told you to finish what you started!" He kisses her face slowly and moves his hands on her body. She felt violated as she whimpered for him to stop. He whispered in her ear, "You belong to me now. If you cross me, I will have your daughter too! You said she's sixteen now, is that right?" He let out this heinous laugh.

"No! Please. Not my daughter. PLEASE! Please leave her alone!"

"Well, then we shouldn't have a problem, should we? You see, Chiquita, I always get what I want."

Kat in the Hospital

Kat was still in a coma. As the nurses work on cleaning her tubes, she starts having involuntary movements. Coincidentally, Tootie was assigned to her room. She grabbed the chart before entering the room and sees that her Jane Doe was the unidentified person found at the hotel. She looks at the woman and feels as though she knows her somehow. She can't put her finger on it though as she stared intently trying to make her face out. She rubbed the patient's hair and whispers, "I'm going to get you back on your feet pretty lady!"

Somewhere along I-95 at a service road, Larry gases up the car. As they merge back onto the highway, Larry asks Rico all about this "Eric Morales guy."

Rico lowered his head and said, "He's a bad dude, he's nothing to play with. He offs people as if it's a hobby to him. Like they're nothing, you know? Once, he cut this person's fingers off, one finger for every "G" he owed him."

"Damn. Did he live?"

"I mean…yeah, now they call him 'the finger'."

"Wait…why?"

"He owed Mr. Morales $9,000, so he only had one finger left." They both laughed.

"Damn, good thing he didn't owe him $11,000!" They laughed again hysterically. "So what's next for us?" Larry inquired as the laughter died down.

"We have to be untraceable. No money trails. Nothing that can be traced back to us."

"So we have to spend cash for everything? What happens when our cash runs out?"

Rico takes a deep breath, "Okay, so that's what I need to talk to you about. We, meaning Eric Morales' crew, had a ring. We had girls working for us. Basically, all of the money comes directly back to us. Eric pays us and keeps the rest. The girls get clothes, hair, and nails done. Other than those expenses, it's all profit."

"Wow. Seriously? So how much could we make if we had twenty girls?"

"Anywhere from $8,000 to $10,000 a day, that's at least $40 a customer…you figure, with each girl getting an average of 10 customers per day…for 20 women. But…we have to find kids and promise them the world. We'll eventually take it all back.

Kick their asses; and put them in their place. We have to control them so they can make money for us."

"Oh you know I can handle that!" They laughed again. "Yeah, I know. You beat Shae's ass so bad she couldn't see for two weeks. How long was she in the hospital?"

"I did, didn't I? Ha! Let's see...including rehab...she was in there two months."

"Damn! That's incredible.... Listen, don't call anyone anymore and don't tell anyone where you are. Change your number and we'll get through in other ways."

"Where are we headed?"

"South. Just keep driving." Rico's gaze was fixed on the pavement.

"Okay. So where are we going to find the people?"

"That's the easiest part. Truck stops, bus terminals, foster homes, or juvenile facilities. Anywhere. We'll get them, don't worry. Kids are easy targets, all you have to do is boost their ego's, gain their trust, and we got them!" Larry turned on his radio to his favorite rock station and shook his head in approval as they continued driving.

Chapter 15

Quianna's Story

The night sky in Malibu is beautiful as Armon and Quianna sit poolside, overlooking the vineyard. Quianna is fantasizing about what her life could have been like if she wasn't in this situation, she could have never imagined her life taking this road. But here she was, thousands of miles away from home, sitting in her client's villa next to Mr. "Winery" who happened to have a fancy name to go with his fancy home. Armon Vasquell, the famous vintner and socialite.

Quianna broke the silence, "How long have you been in the vineyard business?"

"It was passed down through five generations and I had to keep the legacy going. I worked very hard at it. Very hard to maintain our brand and reputation."

"Do you have any children to pass it down to?"

"No, I don't. I guess…I haven't found the right woman yet." Quianna looked at him and thought, 'You haven't found the right one yet because you keep buying prostitutes!'

"So, how will you pass down your legacy if you don't have any children?"

"I always planned on it, but I've been too busy running the family business. I really haven't had time for a relationship. I would meet women briefly and then move on."

Quianna looks away and says to herself, "How long will I be here?"

She begins to think about her mom. She felt free enough to express her feelings to Armon about what's going on in her life, now that they've spent some extensive time together. "My mom is probably going crazy right about now. I've been gone so long. She loves me and I know she's missing me. Can I call her?"

"Ehh...I don't know about that. She cannot be missing you pretty lady." He paused for a moment and then says, "She sold you!"

"What?! No, she didn't! How can you say that? You don't even know my mother!" Quianna pushed herself onto the ledge of the pool, angry that she even asked him at all.

"Here, please, get my phone. I will show you the text messages between Quinn and that Karate man. Your mother was given $10,000 for you."

Suddenly, Quianna felt sick to her stomach, as if someone had just sucker punched her. She jumps up from the side of the pool to get the phone. She gives it to Armon with tears falling from her eyes, praying still that he was lying to her. Armon dried his hands on a towel near the chair and scrolled through his phone to a forwarded message between Quinn and Chan, the karate teacher about the sale. Then there was another message to Quinn after Chan delivered the money to Tootie. Quianna was blown away, as she read the messages out loud in total disbelief and started sobbing openly with her towel over her face.

Armon sat in the chair with very little compassion as he watched her cry. Then, without hesitation, he excused himself to go the bathroom. While he was gone, she had time to think. It had been a few days with only weed and wine in her system. Her head was finally clear as she hadn't been given any hard drugs. The housekeeper entered the pool area with a white towel over her arm. She wore white tennis shoes on her feet and a short black and white uniform and spoke with a Spanish accent. She looked like she could have been in her forties, too cute to be doing this kind of work.

The housekeeper saw her and asked, "Ms. Quianna, are you okay, momma. Is there anything I can get you before I leave?"

She wasn't fooled one bit by Quianna's crying. She looked as if she had seen this play out many times before. Quianna asks, "What time are you leaving?"

"In about an hour."

"Well then, we'll have two long Island Iced teas and two new glasses please," as she hands her the old ones. The housekeeper leaves the pool area to get the drinks. Quianna got an idea, it was now or never. She realized, then, that this may be her last chance at an escape. Her mind raced as she experienced an intense adrenaline rush sitting on the side of the pool. She grabbed the bottle of Moscato and turned it up, contemplating her next move. She gets up from out of the pool and Armon returned.

"Is everything okay, why did you get out?"

Quianna replied, "I just have to use the bathroom."

"Very well."

Quianna proceeded through the French glass doors that opened into the great room. She's sweating profusely as she goes directly to the master bedroom and stands in the mirror. She starts pacing back and forth, then, hastily opened his medicine cabinet to find several bottles of prescription meds. The first one she grabbed was Nitroglycerin, but it's a liquid that looks like cough syrup. The next bottle was labeled Xanax. She looks for something to crush the pills, grabs the toilet paper roll, and crushes three pills in the cough syrup. She thought this would surely knock him out, so she can get away. She emptied another bottle of pills in the toilet, pours in the cough syrup and adds the crushed pills. Then, she wiped the counter quickly as time was passing by and it probably seemed longer than a bathroom break. She hid the pill bottle in her bathing suit bottoms and walked back through the house. She sees her pocketbook on the chair. The contents are few but it's hers: two sanitary pads, gum, Chapstick, lipgloss, three red jolly ranchers and a travel size toothbrush and toothpaste kit.

She makes it to the lanai and greets Armon with a kiss on the forehead. The housekeeper brought out the drinks on a silver tray with crackers, cheese, and grapes.

"Mr. Armon, is there anything else you will need? I'm going to clean up, sir and I will see you in the morning."

"I'm fine, have a nice evening."

While the housekeeper walked away, Quianna turned Armon's attention to the sky and blocks his view of the drinks, mentioning how beautiful the moon is. Her time is short, and her plan has to be perfect. She poured the syrup into his drink and stirred it with the glass stirrer. She fixes him a plate of crackers, cheese, and grapes. One by one she picks off the grapes and feeds it to him as she's gazing at the beautiful moon. Armon asked, "Where are the drinks?"

"Oh, of course, I will get them." She's nervously hoping he's not able to taste the medicine in it.

"Bagh! What is this? It's horrible I don't like it! I'm going to tell Sandra never make this again." They laughed.

"It's a Long Island Iced tea. You'll get used to the taste. Take another sip. Let's turn up!"

The housekeeper shut the blinds with her pocketbook on her arm, getting ready to leave. But Quianna is anxious and can't wait. She's desperately watching the time; she wants to leave. Grabbing her wrap around, she slips her feet into her rhinestone sandals. Her nerves are out of control and she's desperate. Time is not on her side, so she changes her plans in a split second. She looked around, then looks over at the cheese tray and grabs the knife. She walked to the edge of the pool, grabbed Armon by his hair, pulled his head back and slit his throat. He begins to gurgle, but she grabbed his towel quickly and covered his mouth, so as to not call attention.

After releasing him into the pool, she took the knife with her, ran across the lanai to the chaise, grabs money from his shorts, and washes the blood from her hands and the knife in the fountain. Quainna heads around the landscaping and sneaks into the garage, hiding in the housekeeper's back seat quietly. The housekeeper closed the side door, got in her car and pulled out the driveway and proceeded to the CA Route 1 ramp. She's blasting Pit Bulls' song, El Taxi. She gets off at Lincoln Blvd to Santa Monica to go to the store.

Quianna gets out, dumps the knife in a garbage can, fixes herself, and blends in with the crowd outside the store. She counts the money, $621. She needed clothes, so she starts looking around. She felt free and unbothered by the fact that she had just murdered someone. Her life had changed dramatically, from living at home with her mother who never had any time for her to being trafficked, and now, to murder. Everything she had lived through up until this moment seemed surreal. Still numb from the fact that her mother sold her, she couldn't stop thinking about the nerve her mom had. All of this from her trying to cut school.

She sat on the brick half wall next to one of the stores trying to collect her thoughts and contemplate her next move. Tears ran down her face as she thought, 'I don't want to call my mom. How could I? The bitch freaking sold me. Like I'm some piece of furniture. She just got rid of me!' Memories of how her mom never came to support her when she got awards in her karate matches flooded her mind. Suddenly, her whole mood changed, 'I hate her! How could she do this to me? How could she sell her own flesh and blood?' She wiped her tears, patted her face, and jumped off the wall, walking down the street. It was getting dark and she needed to find a place to sleep.

She sees a woman on the streets and asks her for directions to the closest hotel. The woman points her in the right direction, and Quianna makes her way, but after a while it seemed to be too far to walk. So, she caught a cab to the motel. As she proceeds to check-in, they asked her for identification. "Why do you need my I.D.? I have money," Quianna insisted.

The hotel clerk responds, "Sorry. No I.D. No room."

"But I need somewhere to sleep tonight. I'm tired!" As she looks down at her hand on the counter, she noticed dried blood on her wrist. She put her arm to her side and pleaded with the clerk to help her out. Quianna then resorts to flirting, "Hey, listen, let me take care of you, honey, and then you can take care of me by letting me get a room. I'll pay!"

"No! No I.D. no stay!"

"So, I guess you don't want a good time tonight. Why don't you let me stay with you in your room? I promise I'll be gone in the morning." The clerk denies her once again. She rolled her eyes at him and headed out the door. The bell rings over the door as she walked out and headed for the parking lot. The bells rings again and the clerk runs out. "Miss! Lady! Okay, you can stay here."

Quianna never looked back, heading across the parking lot with food on her mind. In her view was a Chinese Restaurant two blocks down, hearing the whistles as she sashayed down the street with a yellow bathing suit top and a purple wrap around skirt, her silky black hair flowed with every step she took. A black BMW Z4 sat in front of the store with silver rims, clean and ready. She glanced in, music was blasting but there was no driver. She approaches the counter and checks out the menu. Out of the bathroom comes this nicely built, tall, dark skinned brother. They check each other out and before he can open his mouth…

"Hey handsome!" He leans in close to her at the counter and responds, "What's up sexy?"

"Just enjoying the night. What about you?"

"Oh really, I like to enjoy the night. I could use some company. You want to take a ride?"

Fearlessly, she agreed to go, thinking what can go wrong. After all, nothing could be worse than what she's already experienced. "Sure, let me get my food." She orders the shrimp and broccoli with an egg roll to go. She didn't know he had already been checking her out from his rearview mirror as she approached the restaurant. His order was ready, so he pays and tells her that he'll be in the car, pointing to the black BMW Z4 she so admired. Her order is now ready as well. She heads out the door to the beamer and the fine chocolate brother in the driver's seat. He opens the door from the inside for her and she climbs in. "So, what's your name, handsome?"

"Toddy. Where you comin' from?"

"Uh…don't you want to know my name?"

"I already know it. It's sexy!"

"Ha…nice. No, actually, it's Quianna." They laughed and she continued, "I'm trying to get a hotel room, but I misplaced my I.D. So, I'm having a hard time getting one."

"You got money?"

"Excuse me, um…yeah I do!" She says with attitude wondering whether he was planning to rob her or pay her way.

"Okay, okay…don't bite my head off!" They laughed again and headed for the hotel. "Listen, I'll put it in my name, you can pay for it, sound good?" "Thanks man! I'm so tired. I need a nap. It's been a long day for me." Toddy asked, "Don't you have any bags?"

"No! No, I uh…had to leave in a hurry. I was having boyfriend troubles."

"So, you don't have a boyfriend anymore?"

Quianna frowned, "He's dead to me now!" Toddy pulls out a joint and asks if she wanted some. She smiled and reached for it. When they arrive at the hotel, they both get out simultaneously. He opened the hotel door for her, and they get the room. She paid two hundred and fifty dollars for a 3-night stay. And they both head out to find the room.

As Toddy walks her to her door, Quianna says, "Thank you! Are you going to keep me company?"

"Yeah, I can do that. Most definitely. Just let me get my box out of the car."

"Okay, I'm going to freshen up."

Toddy tells her to leave the door unlocked while Quianna takes a shower. Toddy went back out to the parking lot to get his box, which contains his stash of weed. When he gets back in the room, Quianna yells, "I'll be right out," sticking her head out of the bathroom door, smiling. "I'll be right here!" Toddy replied as he rolls a joint.

She doesn't have any other clothes, so she wears her wrap around as a sundress. She enters the bed area looking more radiant than before. "Toddy, I need a favor if you can." Toddy asked, "What's that?"

"I need some clothes. Can you take me to get something tomorrow?"

"I'll see what I can do." She replies with a bit of an attitude, "If you can, if not I can catch a cab."

"Relax, sexy. I got you," Toddy smirked as he laid back on the bed.

Chapter 16

Jean's Desperation

At the Crown Plaza, Jean is desperate to get out of the penthouse suite. She was afraid of Mr. Morales and didn't know if she was going to be his next victim. She doesn't even want to imagine. From the rumors about his court case to his ability to get rid of anyone who crossed him. 'How long is he going to keep me here?' she thought, trying not to cry. Mr. Morales walks in the bedroom orders her to take off her clothes.

"Please! Please, can I just go home?" She pleads with him in distress.

"Yes…yes of course, you can go. I'll just send for your daughter instead. Eh? I'll have her tricking for me like the other little girls. What do you think? Yes you can go. I will call a ride for you."

"No, no wait. Please, wait, not my baby girl!"

Morales picks up the phone and calls an Uber for Jean. Then, he makes a second call to Sosa and instructs him to get Jean's daughter and bring her to him. Jean is frantic as she listens to the conversation and starts grabbing onto his pants, begging and pleading with him to take her instead.

She begins removing her clothes as she reveals her black laced bra and matching panties.

Morales finished his call, threw her on the bed, and had his way with her. Jean laid there, staring at a painting hung on the side wall, powerless as the tears ran down the side of her face and soaked the pillowcase beneath her head. She felt nauseous and disgusted hearing him grunt with pleasure, feeling his body pressed up against hers. He kissed her neck and face, his breath reeking of cigar and alcohol. That enticing smell of his cologne from earlier that evening had worn off. All she could think was, 'I'm doing this for my baby girl, so he won't take her.' As she focuses on her daughter, she realizes that he was the one responsible for taking the girls that are missing. She is horrified, even more, by the realization that he meant what he said. 'Oh my God. He's really going to go after Te'nah! He won't get my daughter. I will kill him first,' her thoughts lingered. Morales grunted one more time as he relieved himself inside of her.

He rolled over to the side and laid there for a second before yelling, "Get up bitch and get out! Your ride is coming. Pack your daughter's bags too. She probably has soft skin like yours huh! She's sixteen, right? Young just like I like them. Perfect."

Jean cried out, "What? No! Why would you take my child after all I've done for you? Helping you to find your wife and your men. I gave in and did what you said...why are you doing this to me?"

"You haven't done anything for me. I paid you." He walks over to the table and gets the three hundred dollars he had given her earlier. "Now you're only getting a hundred dollars you cheap whore! Get out of my hotel and wait outside in the rain! You're not even worth standing in the lobby."

Jean gets up, weeping uncontrollably, and gets dressed, with her money and her heart in her hand. She's deadened by the turn of events as she rides the elevator to the lobby level. Stepping out of the elevator, she wiped her eyes and took a deep breath, marching past the front desk where she heard "Have a good evening." But she never turned around or even acknowledged the remark. Jean heads for the hotel doors and leans on the building as the rain runs down her head and over her face, staring blankly into the black of the night. The uber driver beeps several times before Jean snaps out of it and realizes it's her ride. She got in the car and the driver called her by her name. She barely got a nod out. He asked her how she was doing, but she just sat up against the car door, motionless. He looked at her, shook his head and pulled off heading to Jersey for the hour ride.

Mr. Tony's Bodega

The NPD and FBI came to Mr. Tony's store to issue a warrant for Rico's arrest. Officer Miller opened the door and asked, "Is Rico Mercado here?" Mr. Tony looked up from his counter and answered, "No, officer. I haven't seen him in a week."

"We have a warrant for his arrest. Where can we find him?"

"I'm sorry, I'm not sure. What's he charged with?"

"Endangering the welfare of a child with multiple counts. We need to find him. Do you have any idea where he could be? Do you have a phone number for him?"

"About a week ago he called me but now he's not answering, so I just keep calling." Officer Miller cuts in saying, "Give us that number." Mr. Tony tells them everything he knows. Officer Miller instructs him to give them a call if he hear from Rico. She hands Mr. Tony her card and the cops leave. Mr. Tony is now more worried than ever. 'I have to find Rico!' He thinks to himself. Then, calls back to Puerto Rico to find out if anyone had heard from him, but no one had.

Across the street, Sosa went to find Te'nah. He waited hours but to no avail, so he leaves. Jean was back in Jersey and glad to be home, away from Eric Morales. She kept replaying the evening and the horrible scenes in her head over and over again. She didn't know if that was rape or if it was consensual since she gave it up to save her daughter. Once she was in the house her anxiety turned to anger. She contemplated ways to kill Eric Morales. His team was falling apart, and this would be a great time to get rid of him. Jean's thoughts consumed her, standing sluggishly from the Vicodin she had taken. Her phone rang, it was Te'nah. Jean's words were slow and her voice groggy.

Te'nah replied, "You don't sound good mom, I'm coming home." "No! STAY WHERE YOU ARE! There's someone trying to kidnap you like they did the other girls. He told me that they are coming for you," Jean warned her daughter.

"You know who kidnapped them? Call the cops!"

"No, not exactly. I have to talk to you in the morning. Promise me you won't come home. Stay at your dad's. Okay?"

"Okay, I promise, I love you mom!"

"I love you too. Listen, I might have to send you away for a bit. Don't go to school. I will make some calls to get you out. Don't walk the streets. I mean it, Te'nah!"

"Are they the same guys that went into Ms. Kat's house? I called the cops. They were arrested."

"Oh my God, I didn't know you were the one who called the cops. Good, I'm glad. Good job Nae! Now, do as I told you. I love you baby."

Vivian's Story

Vivian went over to Mr. Willie's house and rang the bell. Mr. Willie came to the door, "Who is it?"

"It's Vivian."

"Come in Viv. What's going on?"

"They found Sheeka! She's in Atlanta! I didn't have the money to get there and pick her up. But, they said they could arrange to bring her home! I want to be happy, but I'm confused Mr. Willie. She didn't seem like my child. She was cussing at me and she was very angry. The officer said she was on drugs. She's only twelve! I need prayer. Can you pray with me?"

"Sure I can. Let me say this. God has rescued your child. She is safe and most importantly ALIVE! God is able to fix those other things. At least you have your child back. Prepare your other children for her coming home. Let them know she's not going to be the same. But she is home again."

Vivian agrees with Mr. Willie as she begins to cry in his arms. He holds her hands to pray, "God, we thank you for Sheeka & Vivian that they will be reunited. We thank you that Sheeka is safe and you've kept her through this rough time. God help this mother to receive her child with open arms, no matter the situation and circumstances. Help them to heal and trust you for the rest. Give Vivian strength to deal with everything she's about to face, in Jesus name. Amen."

"Thank you!" She wiped her eyes and as they are walking to the door they hear a knock. It was Shae.

"Hey Shae!" Mr. Willie gives her a hug, then Vivian pops out from behind him. They scream, happy to see each other. Across the street Boots hears all the commotion so he comes out from the alley.

Boots hollered, "Hey what's going on over there?" Laughing and walking over towards the group. It's raining heavily now, so Mr. Willie invited everyone into the house. They head for his living room where they all sat down to talk. Mr. Willie asked, "So Vivian does everyone know the good news?" Vivian takes a breath and shouts, "They found Sheeka!"

Shae exclaimed, "Oh thank God! How is she? Is she okay? Is she home?" Vivian teared up, "She's on drugs. They gave my baby drugs, Shae!"

Boots added, "Vivian, she can get help. Let's just thank God, she is alive!" Boots walked to the window, not wanting anyone to see him getting emotional. He burst out yelling, "Thank you Jesus! Thank you Jesus!" Crying openly.

Mr. Willie walks over, rubs his back, and praises God with him. Shae and Vivian just sit quietly, taking it all in. Boots got himself together and sat back down.

Mr. Willie, still standing at the window, asked, "Why was the police across the street yesterday?" Boots tells him about the men who broke into Kat's apartment. "I think she might be on the run because they can't find her. Jean don't even know where she's at." "Now you know it's for real 'cause she knows everything!" said Shae.

"It's a lot of crazy stuff happening around here, the girls missing; Tony's nephew behind this and he's gone, Kat is missing too. What in the hell is going on? It's too much," Boots remarked.

"I heard Nia was found too. We are only waiting for Quianna to be found. Has anyone heard anything about her?" Shae asked.

Boots jumped in, "No and Tootie's taking it too well. She doesn't even act as if anything happened anymore."

Mr. Willie thinks back and agrees, "Yes, I noticed that as well. I guess everybody expresses their feelings differently. You know, it was strange. The police came in the cleaners and asked me if I knew Tootie and if I knew when Quianna was born?" "So what you say?" asked Boots.

"Well, I told them when she moved here the little girl was a small child. Didn't really know when she was born."

Boots replied, "They asked me the same thing. They asked me if I knew her father. Quianna is going to have a birthday in a couple of weeks. She always spent her birthday with me. If she was out of town, she'd always call me on the phone."

Vivian chimed in, "Boots you raised that little girl. Tootie never had no time for her. Always working. That little girl was fond of you, Boots."

"Yeah, that's my baby, I miss her. When she was little, she used to say they moved around a lot and she hoped she could stay here forever."

Mr. Willie commented, "Yeah I think they moved from different states because of Tootie's job. You know in all the years I have known them I have never seen any family of theirs. Not even a boyfriend of Tootie's. Nothing."

"Well…I think that Chan guy likes her," Boots scoffed.

Shae asked, "So where do you think Kat is? Wow! I hope she is okay. Do you know these guys who broke into her apartment?"

Boots described them as tall, Latino, well-dressed businessmen. Vivian gets up and announces that she has to go. "Please pray for my daughter, please. Good night ya'll." Everyone agreed to pray, and one by one they left Mr. Willie's.

Chapter 17

Tootie and Chan

About a month before Quianna was kidnapped, Tootie was over Chan's house and had overheard a conversation he was having with Eric Morales. When he was done talking, Tootie asked, "What was that all about? What are you into, Chan Liu?" "I'm a magician. I make people disappear!" Chan waved his hands as if casting a spell. Half-smiling at his joke, Tootie sighed and looked a bit worried. "What's wrong? You need me to make someone disappear?" He laughed at his joke heartily. Tootie gets comfortable in his arms for some sort of security.

"Yesterday the F.B.I. called the hospital asking human resources for information about me. I wasn't at work yet, but the H.R. rep left me a note. They wanted a call back. I have to get out of here or they'll find us, and they'll find…never mind. We'll talk later about it. I'm going to need some money, Chan. Can you help me?"

Chan was concerned, "You're not going to leave me, are you? I got you babe. You know that." He rolled over top of her, nibbling at her face. She screamed with laughter. "Is this about…?" Tootie cut him off, "Yes. I can't risk going away for what I did. If they figure out…"

"So, you need money, and you need a solution. What if I could give you both? What if I had a way to make her and it all go away? I don't want you to leave, so maybe you don't have to…I know what to do. I got you, baby. I'll take it from here." Chan wrapped his arm around Tootie and reassured her with a kiss on the forehead.

Nia and Renee's Reunion

In New York, when Nia was reunited with her mom, they ran into each other's arms crying and embracing one another. The officer told Renee she could join Nia in the conference room. They both walked into the conference room and took a seat at the large table, Renee looked at her daughter, realizing her twelve-year-old child wasn't the same person that left her home some months ago. She looked like she had aged. She wasn't the sweet mild-mannered child she'd known.

Renee broke her silence, "So what happened, Nia?"

"Sheeka asked me if I wanted to go to Coney Island with Mr. Tony's nephew. I didn't want to go. I didn't want to go mom, I swear!" She started crying. With her nerves on edge, she continued, "She said that he would give us fifty dollars. I wanted the money so I could buy some new clothes, so...."

"New clothes? Are you kidding me? New clothes? Are you crazy? You mean to tell me you were kidnapped over fifty dollars? I should kick your ass right now! Nia, how dumb could you be?"

"What? Are you serious? Kick my ass?" She pushed back from the table, angry as hell. "What's wrong with you? My ass was prostituted out, drugged out, raped...and your ass is worrying about me not going to school! You don't think I've been punished enough? Yes...I wanted the money because your ass is always broke. You never have any damn money. Yeah I needed the money!"

Renee's mouth flew open in total shock as she paused to take a breath. "I'm sorry! Honey, I'm so sorry. You're right. I should have been more considerate of how you're feeling and what you've been through." They both started crying and the officers entered the room. Detective Rouse asked Renee if they could go to a family member's house or be placed in protective custody. He said, "We need to know what you'd like to do. At this time it's not recommended to go back to your home.

We're not sure of Rico's location. It can be very dangerous."

He proceeded to tell Renee that Nia couldn't come home for safety reasons. The police couldn't secure Rico's location so Renee and her family would have to relocate for now. She was told not to tell anyone about her whereabouts, not even family. They'd have to go into a Protective Witness Program for their safety. After hearing Nia's story, the FBI investigation went nationwide. The FBI had discovered that this ring originated in Puerto Rico. It was now in the U.S. and crossing state lines fast. Their objective was to catch this ring at the head.

Quianna in Santa Monica

Quianna used Toddy's phone to call Ricky. Ricky looked at the strange 424 number on his phone and answered hesitantly, "Yeah? Who this?"

Quianna yelled, "What up slick Rick!" "Key?!" It had been a while, but he recognized her voice instantly.

"Who else calls you slick Rick?"

"Yo! What's up baby you aight? Where are you, where have you been? Yo, it's crazy around here. Did that dude Rico take yo ass? What happened?"
"Yeah that punk motherfucker. Listen, I don't have a lot of time, can you send money? I'm on the run and my funds are getting low. Yo, and don't tell nobody you heard from me either. Especially my mother!" He cuts her off, "Wait…not even your mother? Key, what kind of shit is that? You don't even sound like the same chick. You sound all grown and shit. What the nigga do to you Key? I'm gonna put one in his ass when I see him for real."

"Enough of that. Let me ask you a question. How has my mom been?"

"She's good. We don't see her much. They're remodeling y'alls apartment so she's at the hotel. She goes to work like normal. The police are thick around there though. We had to move our spot. But they been askin' a lot of questions about you and your moms. Like more than the other girls, it was weird. Yo, you know they found Sheeka and Nia? They should be coming home any day now, I think. They said Sheeka is strung out and shit."

"OMG, no." Quianna started crying, though she was still happy that the girls were found and they were able to get away from those horrible people.

Then she continued, "Listen answer my question. Does my moms act as if she cares that I'm missing? Be one hundred with me, you won't hurt my feelings."

"Hmm…you know I never thought about it, but honestly…no. I mean, she was coming and going as usual. One day your karate teacher was talking to her and he gave her a white envelope. While he was talking she busted out crying and Boots went over to see if she was alright. But I don't even think she took off from work. Ronnie noticed it because she always had her scrubs on. I think she went back the day after you went missing, now that I think of it."

"Damn! Huh…I can't believe it. Yeah, that bitch sold me to the kidnappers, real shit Ricky! Her own daughter!"

"What!!!! Yo are you for real?"

"Look I told you I can't talk long. I'm on somebody's phone but I will call you back on a prepaid. Don't tell ANYBODY SHIT!"

"Where you at, I'll come get you Key!"

"I need money now to survive and I don't have anywhere to stay. I'm in a hotel for the night but that's not going to last long. I'll call you back soon!"

"Okay…but, where you at Key?"

"California."

"Give me your exact info. I'll come get you baby!" Quianna gave him the name of the hotel she was at. He said, "I'm gonna book a flight. I'm coming for you baby. Don't worry! I got you." "Thanks," she replied, "but don't tell anyone your coming for me." Ricky assured her he wouldn't, though Ronnie had heard the conversation, and when the call ended, he booked a flight from Newark to LAX.

At the hotel, Mr. Morales and the men who were after Rico enter the living room area. Mr. Morales asked, "Well. Where is Rico?" The guard replied, "We can't find him, jefe. It's like he knew we were coming for him and he disappeared. His phone was left at the house. I wonder how he knew we were after him."

Morales was pissed and threatened him. "Yea, how did he know?! He did not just quit the business and he is not a mind reader! Someone is giving him information!" The angrier he gets, the heavier his Spanish accent becomes. "If you can't find him, go see the uncle. If he doesn't help you, kill him! Go now and don't come back here until you find him!" Slamming his drink on the table, he breaks the glass. Now, he's pacing around the suite and goes on with his rant, "Escuchame bien...I better get results! Since I've been here, everything has gone wrong! My wife is missing, no one can find her. Rico is missing, no one can find him. Two of my men get locked up and now are being deported. That girl gets taken and it turned out her mom stole her ass, so now the FBI is coming close to MY operation!! I'm getting ready to make all you guys disappear like those witnesses because you idiots might run your mouths to the policia! Three days! You have three days to come back with answers, or it's your ass!"

Mr. Tony walked over to the 'Bricks' to Jean's apartment. She opens the door slightly to greet him, "Hey, Tony." He returns the greeting, "Hello Jean! Are you okay?" He noticed she didn't look well. Jean answered, "Yeah, I'm fine, just a little under the weather, that's all. What's up?"

"Okay. I need you and Te'nah to watch the store for about a week, do you think you'd still be able to help me?"

"Te'nah is away. She won't be back for about two weeks."

"Well...maybe I can get Bett to help you. Have you seen her?"

"No, but I can call Shae, she'll get her to help me."
Tony was relieved, "Yes. Can you call her please?
I'd like to start training you guys. I have to leave
town on an emergency." She assured him she'd
call, and Mr. Tony thanked her. "I really
appreciate this. If you weren't able to do it, I'd
have to close the store down until I got back." "No
problem Tony." He left and headed back to the
store.

Jean grabbed her phone to call Te'nah, "Hey
sweetie, listen. You have to leave town, I'm
coming to get you. Be ready, I'm bringing your
clothes. We have to go to Aunt Julie's house
now!" Te'nah was worried and replied, "Okay
mom, but please tell me what's going on? You're
scaring me!"

"I'll explain everything to you when I get there but
you have to promise me that you won't tell anyone
where you're going. If you do, others will find us,
and they will kill us. Promise me!"

"Okay. I promise." "Let me handle something and
I'm on my way!" Jean then called Shae, and Bett
was with her. They made plans to meet at Mr.
Tony's store for training.

Rev. Briggs was over at the church. The weather
was terrible; stormy all day, raining hard with loud
thunder and lightning. Some streets were

beginning to flood. He was there waiting for Nia and Renee to arrive before they left for their undisclosed location. Pacing back and forth in the sanctuary, he prayed for the girls. "Father, I thank you that your powerful hand has kept our girls. I thank you for Nia and Sheeka being snatched from the hands of the enemy. You have heard our prayers Lord. We need you to bring one more of our precious girls, Quianna, home. Keep her safe and cover her with your blood. Give her a way of escape and direct her path. Bring her home God, in Jesus' name." He waited a while longer, but they never showed up, so he went home.

Renee Chooses Her Family

Renee was faced with the tough decision to uproot her children and the life that she's known for years. She was afraid she would have to leave her job and pull her kids from their schools. Especially since Renee had just became a supervisor at the Newark International Airport. She had been waiting on the job promotion for over a year now and had only been in her new position for a month. How could she quit? But she took serious consideration of what the officer said about the sex traffickers and the possibly of them coming back for Nia. Renee started crying as she was about to make a life changing decision. Never to see her family again, but she understood her kids had to come first and Nia had been through enough! Before she leaves, the agent asked her about her decision. Then, she considered the possibility of moving away and working at another location, where the environment would be best for Nia. 'That might be the best way to go, new school, new life, and new friends,' Renee thought. She decided to let the agency provide a protective custody for her family.

Renee is told Nia of her decision to relocate under the Witness Protection Program. Nia agreed and wanted to move out of state. Renee hadn't planned on exactly that but understood her daughter had to come first. She stepped out to make a call to her manager. Shortly after, Renee returned with a look of relief on her face, "Nia, baby, I just got done speaking to my manager and the federal agents. We're going into protective custody. And I'll still be able to work for the airport just not in New Jersey." Nia looked at her mom confused, then looked at Agent Wilson. Agent Wilson interjected, "You and your family will be moving to California. You will get new identities and, luckily, your mom will be able to work at LAX. Of course, no one there will know who she really is and there will be no ties to her current employment in Newark. But it was good that we were able to resolve this matter promptly. Right now, we're working on your documents and transportation. Unfortunately, we'll have to move quickly." Nia was both nervous and relieved that they were moving far away from the East Coast. Everything there now reminded her of the horror she had lived. Renee had planned on passing by Rev. Briggs' church for prayer, but the urgency of the matter made that impossible. From here on out, all communication with past relationships would be cut off.

Rico and Larry arrived at a truck stop in NE Maryland off I-95. They pulled in and it was like money in the bank. They parked and watched women going from truck to truck, knocking on doors, asking truckers if they wanted any sexual favors. They watch carefully to see if the girls had pimps around. They continued observing, then Larry had to pee and couldn't hold it any longer. But Rico was on top of his game. He thought, 'I'm back in business. Look at all this ass out here!' Larry goes to the bathroom passing two young ladies with booty shorts on in mid-September. Although it was still warm, you can clearly see they were hookers. Rico realized that they were renegades; in business for themselves. So he checked his 'stash, then licked his fingers to run them across his eyebrows as he checked himself in the mirror before getting out to put on his best game.

Before Larry comes out of the bathroom, Rico observes a confrontation between one of the girls and a truck driver. She jumped on the step and banged on the truck door. Cussing out the driver, she threw her shoe at his window, went over to the landscaping and grabbed several rocks. She starts throwing them at the truck's window and the driver got out and grabbed her arm. He hurled her to the ground before she could throw anything else. Seeing this, Rico ran over and slammed the driver against his truck before he hurt her. Rico threatens the driver, "Give her the money before I beat the shit out of you!" He looked at the girl, "How much he owe you?" She replied, "$40." He looked back at the driver and demanded, "Give her $60 for her damn trouble!" The driver reached one hand in his pocket and threw $60 on the ground, he got back in his truck and left.

Looking concerned, Rico asked, "You okay baby girl?" She eyes him up and down and says, "Yeah, thank you. What's your name?" "Rico." He helped her up off the ground. "You didn't have to do that. They always pull that shit!" She brushed some dirt off and Rico played on her emotions, "Are all the girls together? Y'all don't have no security?" She lets her guard down and tells him, "No, we don't but we're alright." Rico saw his opportunity and asked if they wanted to travel with them because they're headed to make some big money. He told her he could protect them from those types of creeps and provide everything for them; a place to sleep, food, clothes. He promised her, "I'll take care of you baby girl. And you won't have to worry about a thing." He told her to talk it over with her girls and let them know because they were headed south. Larry then joins Rico. The girl asked, "How much we get paid?" Rico explained, "Half of what we charge." They continued their conversation and agreed to go with them. Rico introduced Larry and explained that they'd be their security. There were six girls, but only four agreed to go with them.

Rico tells them that they were headed to Atlanta and it was time to go. They stood around waiting to get into Larry's car. Rico promised them they were going to make a lot of money together and that he was going to get them in the Atlanta clubs. He also told them that he was going to buy them some nice clothes and get their hair and nails done. The girls listened intently to all his promises when Rico changes the conversation to explain that there are rules. He laid out the rules, "One, you have to wash. Two, your clothes must be clean. Three, you can't look drugged out. Four, you have to keep your weight up. Five, you can't steal from your clients. Six, you have to be honest and listen to me and Larry. If you don't, you have to leave and it won't be good! And seven; and this is the most important rule, you BETTER have all my money. So, are y'all coming with us or not?" One of the girls spoke up, "So what's in it for us again?"

Rico looked at her blankly and said, "You get a place to stay, hot showers, food every night, nails, hair and clothes. But mostly, security, and you will get paid what your clients are asked to pay. Do we have a deal? Oh, and no back talking or any more knocking on truck doors! We're past that." Larry is getting antsy and tells them, "Okay, we need to get out of here! Who's coming? We can only take four so who's it gonna be?" The one girl, Shawna says, "I'm down." Another one, Marva, adds, "I'm in." Jacqui said, "Me too." Lee Lee, a tranny, says, "I want to go!" Larry looked at her and asked, "So who are you?" She tells him, "I'm Lee Lee. I'm a woman with all my man junk. Wanna see?" Larry choked, "No, I believe you!" Larry tells the girls, "Listen, if you get busted, never tell any of the business and we will get you out each and every time. We have to trust you and we will make y'all trust us." Rico says, "Come on ladies, chop chop! We got a long ride." They pile up in the car as Rico puts their book bags and small personal items in the trunk. Larry and Rico talk at the back of the car. Larry questions Rico, "So we are really dealing with a tranny?" Rico tried to reason with him, "This is going to be good man, you'll see. It's going to bring in more money. We are putting together a variety of merchandise. People out there in that world like variety, we lucked out on a good bunch I think." "You think they are going to follow the rules?" "Oh, hell no! We just told them a bunch of lies, we'll beat their asses and have them under our thumbs in no time. Let's go!"

"Hold up. Somebody smells like a dead ass deer! They gots to take showers before they get in my car. I'm not riding to Atlanta with no stankin' cooch in my car!" Rico laughed, "Okay, okay! I hear you! Everybody go wash up in the truck stop and change your clothes. I'll go get y'all something to eat." Larry goes to gas up and, when they were done, they hopped back on the highway.

Chapter 18

One Week Later

Kat was still at the hospital, but the swelling on her face had gone down and she gained consciousness. They moved her from the Trauma Unit to ICU. She's beginning to speak, but her eyesight is still blurry. Tootie was scheduled to work in ICU. She's looking at some charts when she hears from one of the other nurses that their Jane Doe was semi-conscious. Tootie went in the room to see her and was surprised to see that it was one of her good friends. She screamed, "Kat! Oh my God!" She grabbed and kissed Kat's hand and tells a nurse, "I know this lady! I know her!" She turns back to Kat and asked, "Kat, can you hear me? If you can hear me, move one of your fingers!" She's watching, but there was no movement. One of the other nurses who was being relieved by Tootie told her she had just given Kat morphine because she was moaning in pain.

Tootie tried to figure out what happened and thought that Kat probably got robbed for her drugs. The nurse asked her how she knew the patient and Tootie told her that she lives in her building. The nurse says, "Okay, we'll have to tell the Charge

Nurse her name. Woohoo, our patient has a name! Amen!" Tootie agreed and continues trying to get Kat to talk as she rubs her dreads. She gets a warm cloth and washes her face, continuing to talk to her. "Kat, do you know who did this to you? Can you hear me? You're in the hospital. It's Tootie. Kat, you're going to be alright. I'm here with you baby and I won't leave you! If you can hear me, please move your fingers." Kat slowly lifted her index finger and kept it up. Tootie was excited, "Yes! I'm so proud of you! You're going to get up from here. I promise!" She continues to care for her friend, washing her and changing her bandages.

In the interim, Special Agent Daniels called Vivian to inform her of their plans to get Sheeka home. "Mrs. Davis, we're sending Sheeka home with one of our agents. Will you be able to pick her up from Newark International Airport?" Vivian replied, "I don't have any money to come get her. I don't have a ride." Vivian had clearly been drinking. Special Agent Daniels says, "Okay. That's okay, we can bring her to you, what's your address? I do suggest however that you guys move from your residence in case the kidnappers come back for Sheeka, we haven't apprehended everyone involved. We have discussed protective custody." Vivian got upset at this suggestion and interrupted,

"I can't leave. I don't have any money to send her to any of my relatives and I have other kids. I can't just uproot everybody because of this!" Daniels interrupts her, "Ma'am, we are only giving you suggestions. We can't make you leave but you should take this very seriously. Your other children could be at risk if the traffickers return. I just wanted to give you some options. I'd hope you would make the best decision for Sheeka and your other children. She is going to need extensive drug treatment and counseling because of all she's been through."

Vivian, thinking only of herself again, rebuts, "I can't move. I can get welfare to pay for her counseling. We'll work it out, but nobody's gonna uproot everything because she wanted to skip school and then got her ass kidnapped!"

"Mrs. Davis, have you been drinking?" Vivian gets bent out of shape at the question and replies, "Yes, wouldn't you? My life has been turned upside down because of all this shit!"

"How much have you had to drink ma'am?"

"A fifth! Why? That's really none of your damn business!" Daniels kept her composure and adds, "Ma'am, I think we should talk later when you're sober." Vivian gets smart, "I don't care to talk later, just bring my damn daughter home," and she hung up the phone.

Daniels looked at Sheeka and says, "Wow Sheeka. Can you tell me a little about your mother?" Sheeka questioned, "What do you want to know?"

"Well, is she a good mother?" Unsure of what she meant by this, Sheeka replied, "She's cool until she drinks."

"What do you mean by that?"

"When she drinks, she's a crazy woman, a thug, a fighter; not herself. But when she's sober, she's the nicest person you ever want to meet." Daniels laughed and Sheeka was confused at her reaction.

"I'm sorry, but you said she acts like a thug! I wasn't expecting that." They both laughed. "Yeah. It's funny now, but not when it's going on! One time she beat my brother's father up for switching her Vodka with a glass of water. He had a black eye, his nose was bleeding and he had two teeth missing. All over one glass of Vodka. She's totally different, no joke!" Daniels said, "Wow!" This was her way of making Sheeka feeling comfortable with her. They continued talking, Daniels went on, "Has she ever hit ya'll while she was drinking?" Sheeka paused, looking at her like she was crazy, now realizing that she was prying.

She immediately put up her defenses and said, "I'm not doing this with you. You want me to rat on my moms?! Get the hell out of here!"

Daniels tried to calm Sheeka down and assure her that was not what she was doing. "No, we're just having a conversation. I'm sorry. I promise I wasn't going to try to use it against her. I was just curious, because she seemed so angry. This conversation is between you and me." Sheeka didn't trust her, "No, the hell it's not. I've done seen enough Law & Order to know this shit ain't between us. My moms ain't perfect, but she's my moms." The room was silent, and Special Agent Daniels relented from asking any further questions.

Quianna and the Dead Vintner

Ricky arrived at LAX and called Toddy's phone. Toddy picked up, "Hello?" Ricky hesitated a bit and finally says, "Yeah, I'm trying to reach Quianna."

"Hold on. Quianna, someone's on the phone for you. That your boyfriend?" Quianna explained, "No, that's my boy from Jersey, he flew out here to help me." Toddy passed her the phone, and she answered, "Hello?" "I'm here baby. Who's that nigga?"

"Relax. It's my boy Toddy. I just met him, but he helped me get a room."

"You didn't mess with him did you?" Quianna can't believe him, "No, boy! Just get here!" She gives him the address of the hotel and ended the call. Toddy was ear hustling and asked, "So…what…he's coming here?" Quianna, with nothing to hide answered him bluntly, "Yeah." "Oh, I thought we were gonna spend some more time together?" She laid her head on his pillow next to him and said, "We can!" Toddy rubbed her stomach and she rolled toward him for a kiss.

She explained, "But I need to meet up with my boy so he can get me back on track. Give me your number and, when he leaves, I'll call you. But he might be here for a couple of days. You have to let me get situated. I'll call you with my new number." Toddy reluctantly got up to gather his things to leave. "Okay, call me." Five minutes later, he grabbed his box and, before heading out the door, he tells Quianna, "I can help you too, just give me a chance."

"Okay, let me take care of this first, but thanks. I just don't know you like that and he's like family. He's gonna fix this situation and get me on my feet, then I can rock with you."

At the Vasquell Estate in Malibu, the housekeeper, Sandra, arrived to work and found everything just like she left it. She begins to make breakfast as usual. The menu of the day is waffles, strawberries with whipped cream and a sprinkle of blueberries; eggs and coffee. The smell of the food is filling the air and Sandra tried to stay quiet so she didn't wake up Mr. Vasquell. Usually, as soon as he smells coffee, he steps out of the bedroom into the great room that overlooks the mountain with a great view of the ocean below. Sandra typically greets him with a silver tray that holds his coffee, newspaper, and his dipped cigar and lighter. But this morning, thirty minutes had passed by and he wasn't up yet. Sandra opened the blinds to the Lanai and realizes that last night's food and towels were still there.

Finding it strange, she proceeded to clean them up and, as she walked closer to the pool she saw red in the water. Looking further into it, she discovered the pool water wasn't red, it was blood and Mr. Vasquell's body floating in it. She dropped the tray and screamed hysterically, "Oh my God, oh my God!" She ran frantically through the house and out to her car. She started to hyperventilate and bent over to put her head between her legs, trying to get the image of Mr. Vasquell out of her head. It took her about 12 minutes to gain her composure enough to call the police. "9-1-1, what's your emergency?"

"He's dead!" The operator asks, "Who's dead ma'am? Please calm down and tell me what happened." Sandra tried to collect herself, "My…my boss. He's dead in the pool!"

"Where are you? What's the address?" Sandra gave her the address, struggling to get each word out. The operator tried to get as much information as she could, "Ma'am, did he drown? What's his name?" Sandra did her best to answer, "No, I don't think so…there's blood in the pool! His name is Armon Vasquell." "Try to stay calm. The police are on their way." Sandra was numb, sobbing in her car. After about 10 minutes, she heard the sirens blazing. The police pulled up to find the house empty. No one answered the door. Suddenly, the garage door opened, and Sandra ran into the arms of one of the police officers. She couldn't get a word out, all she could do was point to the pool area. The officers went in through the house with guns drawn and found the famous Vintner floating face down in his infinity pool.

In Queens, Eric Morales sat quietly in his hotel suite by himself, which wasn't safe at all, but he had been quiet about his return. He looked over his numbers and realized his escort business was more lucrative than drug trafficking. His wheels were starting to turn as he began to set up his next plan. Eric Morales grabbed his phone and called Scott Grizilla a.k.a. Black Bear, his rival in the business. Morales' wife had been missing for a week now and he was convinced that Black Bear had her since she wasn't in jail or in the hospital. He was unsure if anyone knew he was in town, after all he hadn't left the hotel since he arrived in the city. But if anyone was looking to get him, it would be Black Bear.

Black Bear lived in Jamaica Estates in Queens, NY. As the phone rings, he answered, "Waa gwaan." Mr. Morales shouted, "Bear, you got my wife? I will kill you, don't mess with my property, pendejo!"

Bear responded to the threat, "Ooooh, Bomboclaat! How dare yuh ask dis rude bwoy about yuh long lost wife? Mi had hur before but not now," he laughed. "Mi cyan 'elp yuh wit dat. Yuh here in mi territory huh bwoy?"

"Yeah, I'm here and you better turn her loose. You know I know how to find you, Bear."

"Ha...mi dead wid laugh. So, yuh lost yu Ooman? Silly man! Whey a yuh trafficker? Yuh take lil babies now do yuh eh? Mi will have yu head when mi see yuh. Yuh a ded man walking see? Ya eard meh? Ded! Mi cum and spill yu blood whey yuh be. Yuh betta not be near mi. Told yuh once and now mi tell yuh for de las time. De Black Bear hibernation is ova and me gwonna feast."

"Listen carefully, Bear, I know you have her and you're trying to anger me. You took a warehouse of drugs last year and now my wife. Thirty-two million is nothing, but a day without my wife will make me kill you and your family. Remember I have some of your people and you're still mad about that, huh?" Morales laughed, "They turned on you just like she did. Give me my precious cargo! You mistreated her when you had her, so I showed her what a real man is like."

"Mi don have yu precious cargo, yu hurt over the $32 million mi tek from yuh, dat just paid for yuh tek'in mi ooman. Yuh steal little gyals, huh. Yuh proud a yuhself. Tekin' babies from dey mommas huh! Dey innocent, yu done, yu renk." Bear continued to go off on Morales in Jamaican, "Nuh romp wid mi (Don't mess with me). Mi deh yah, everything criss (see you later)." Black Bear slammed the phone. Eric Morales still had no idea whether Bear had his wife or where she could be. He was no closer to finding her and, after his exchange with Bear, he was fired up.

In Santa Monica, Ricky arrived at the hotel right after Toddy left feeling angry that he had to leave. Toddy didn't take lightly the fact that, in his mind, he was rejected. And what Quianna didn't know was that he also had sociopathic tendencies and control issues that kept him fueled. Ricky and Quianna hugged outside the hotel door and kissed on the lips, as Toddy watched their every move from across the street. Quianna and Ricky went into the hotel and walked arm in arm to her room on the second floor. The curtains were still open, and Toddy could see them as they sat on the bed and talked. Thirty minutes had passed by and Ricky got up to close the blinds. Toddy was furious, though he had just met her, he felt like he lost a battle. Moments later, they both exited the room. They headed to the bus stop to find stores where Quianna could buy some clothes. Toddy calmed down realizing that they didn't have time to make love. 'Maybe he is only a friend', he thought. As they passed by the liquor store, Ricky noticed some guys checking Quianna out. Ricky asked the guy, "You got a problem?" The guy reacted sheepishly, "What?" "You heard me!"

The other guys laughed at their friend and he was embarrassed. He tried to show off, "I'll take your girl if I want, punk!" Ricky clapped back, "And I'll put a hot one in your ass." He didn't have a gun, but in the moment it didn't matter. Suddenly, the guy pulled out his gun and pointed it at Ricky's head. Quianna grabbed the guy's arm and pleaded with him, "Come on now! We don't need no trouble." She smiled and winked at the guy as she spoke. He looked back at her and lowered his gun. Ricky put his hands down and grabbed Quianna around the neck as they walked down the street hugged up. Meanwhile, Toddy was still slowly following them, watching every move. They hopped on the bus safely and headed for the closest Walmart.

On the bus ride, Quianna asked Ricky to call Boots. "You can block your number, but I want to talk to him." Ricky blocked his number, dialed Boots, and passed her the phone. After a few rings, Boots answered, "Hello?" Quianna teared up at the sound of his voice, "Hey Mr. Boots, its Quianna!" Boots was pleasantly surprised to hear her, "Baby girl?! Are you okay? Thank God you're alive!"

"Yes, I'm good. How are you?"

"Good, I'm good...but when are you coming home?" Quianna got quiet, "I'm not."

"What? Why not?"

"Listen, Mr. Boots, I can't explain now, but please do me a favor. I know it's gonna sound crazy but please don't tell my mother that you heard from me." But Boots didn't think it was crazy at all, "Okay, I won't!"

"Wow, really? I'm surprised you're not challenging me on this like you always do."

"Look, your mom ain't right baby girl." Quianna starts choking up, "She sold me Mr. Boots. She...sold...me!" "I know or at least I thought that's how it went down. Never mind, keep in touch with me and if you need money, call me and I'll send it to you."

"But you'll need it for yourself Mr. Boots."

"Baby, I have plenty of money. The pan handling business has been on point!" Quianna laughed, "Okay, love you. When I get a number, I'll call you." Boots asked, "Where you at?" But before he could finish, Quianna ended the call.

Chapter 19

Kat and Tootie

At the hospital, Kat began to slowly regain consciousness. It had been hours since Tootie had seen her so on her lunch break, she went to the TICU to check on her and Kat was now wide awake. Tootie was happy to see her friend had awakened and asked her, "Kat how are you?" Kat replied slowly, "Hi" but was confused about who Tootie was to her. Tootie saw the confusion on her face and tried helping her remember, "Kat, it's Tootie! Your friend, from the 'Bricks'?" Everything came back at once and Kat got excited. She immediately asked for her husband, "Where is my husband?" Tears start running down her face, "Bizzi, get Bizzi for me!" Tootie wiped her tears and started tearing a little herself but had to leave to go finish her break. Tootie thought to herself, 'Wow. Kat is really delusional. She thinks she has a husband!'

New Beginnings and Tragedies

On I-95 South, everyone was piled in Larry's car as they headed from Maryland to Atlanta. Larry asked Lee Lee, "So how'd you get in the game?"

Lee Lee answered, "My mother didn't want no gay son, so she kicked me out when I was 15. I've been surviving on these streets for a year. I saw some ladies tricking and they took me under their wing, and that's how I got in it."

"Shawna. What about you?" He kept the inquiry going. "I ran away because I didn't like school. I couldn't learn as quickly as everybody else, so I kept acting out. My mom kept beating my ass, so I kept running away. Then I met this man and he promised me the world, then tricked me out. I ended up leaving his ass after he almost beat me to death. I caught a bus to Maryland from Atlanta. Ha! Now I'm headed back there. I hope I don't see his ass!" Rico tells her, "Well if you do, he won't be bothering you anymore."

The car was silent for about 10 minutes. Everyone was checking out the scenery while driving down 95, endless fields of green and brown as the fall season approached. Breaking the silence, Marva told her story. "I was molested by my sitter's husband. I became promiscuous at an early age and here I am. I don't want to be doing this shit, but it's all I know. I never had a job at McDonald's like all the kids I grew up with. I was nothing but a whore all my life," she laughed nervously.

Rico responded, "Well, since we're giving out stories, what's yours Jacqui?" "I was raised by my dad, we fell on hard times and his friends used to pay me for sex. I had to help ends meet. Seemed like the only way." Lee Lee asked, "Did your dad know?" Jacqui answered, "No, but later he found out and sent me back to my moms. I stayed there for two weeks and then ran away. I was 15 then. I never went back." Larry probed, "How old are you now?" "Twent-six and my body hurts, I feel old as hell!" Rico asked her, "When was the last time you were checked by a doctor?" "About 7 years ago when I had chlamydia. Then I started making them wear condoms." Rico asked them if they had insurance, to which they all answered no. Rico told them they would get insurance once they get to Atlanta. "In this business, you have to keep yourselves clean and healthy. We're not going to be spreading shit, that's bad for business."

They stopped for a bathroom break in Virginia and Rico decided to check on his uncle. "Hey Uncle Tony, are you okay?" Tony replied, "Nephew, I want to help you." "I'm okay now, don't bother. Are you okay?" Tony told him that the police have a warrant for his arrest on child endangerment charges. He hears the door and tells Rico to hold on so he can see about his customer. Tony put the phone down as two men walked in, dressed in nice black suits but no ties. Tony said, "Hello, can I help you?" One of the men asked if Rico was there. Tony replied, "No, but may I help you with something? I'm his uncle." The man pulled out a gun and pointed it at his head, "Where is Rico?"

"I don't know! Please, please, here...take my money. Take anything. Whatever you want, just don't kill me!"

"We don't want your money! Where's Rico, viejo?" Rico was listening, and Mr. Tony tells them that he's on the phone and hands it to the man who was speaking. He got on the phone and stared at Mr. Tony while he talked, "Where are you?" Rico pleaded, "Listen to me man, I'm close by. I can be there in a few, just give me some time, okay? Just leave my uncle out of this!" Suddenly three loud pops echoed through the phone; there was a gasp of air as Mr. Tony took his last breath.

"Noooooooo! Tio! Tio! No...please!" The second man grabbed the phone quickly and tells Rico, "Your mama will be next, muchacho! Don't make this worse for your family. You better come to us by tomorrow. Or call and say goodbye to your dear mamita! Be at the house in Albany by 3 pm." The men got the number off the caller ID and left the store with the cordless phone. Before getting back in their car, they threw the phone in the sewer down the street. Then they got in the car and drove off. Rico cried as he ended the call.

He called Quinn to let him know that they killed Uncle Tony. Quinn was shocked and started crying. Rico sobbed, "Yo, they're gonna kill mama next if I'm not in Albany by 3 pm, tomorrow. What am I gonna do bro, I'm nowhere near there?" Quinn hesitated for a minute, "Listen, I got another problem. Quianna escaped. I'm not even sure how but I just saw on the news her client was found dead in his pool. I can't get in touch with her." Earlier that day, Quinn had been calling the Vintner but had not gotten an answer. He decided to ride over to the estate to pick up Quianna, but when arrived the L.A. County Sheriff's Department police were onsite. Quinn made a U-turn and had parked down the hill, unsure of what to do. He called the Vintner again and the police answered the phone, he ended the call quickly. The police took the phone as evidence. Quinn wondered if they had Quianna but didn't dare call Eric Morales about another one of his girls missing, especially after what Rico just told him!

Rico stayed quiet but Quinn assured him, "Okay look, I'll call your mom, do they have your number?" "Yes." Quinn tells him that he's going to need to keep in touch with him and not to throw the phone away. "Okay, thanks cuz," he ended to call with an ounce a relief.

Rico was still shaken by what he heard on the phone and walked up to Larry crying about his uncle's death and the threat on his mom's life. "Damn bro. So, are we turning around?" Rico answered in a panic, "Hell no, they will kill me. My cousin is going to move my mom. After we get settled, I'll send for her." "Okay, you ready?" Rico replied, "Yeah, let's just get outta here." They keep heading south. It's dark now so they switched seats and Rico took the wheel for a while. He was nervous and shaking as he drove. In the back of his mind, he knew Eric Morales meant business and it was hard for him to focus. He had to get this money quick before his stash ran out.

On the other side of the country, Quianna and Ricky were headed back to the hotel. They had several bags and had picked up personal items for Quianna along with a suitcase. They arrived at the bus stop where the argument had started, and the same bunch of guys were still hanging out in front of the liquor store. Quianna and Ricky crossed the street towards the hotel. Ricky and the guys stared at each other as he walked but they made it back up to the room without a problem.

They spread out the clothes on the bed and Quianna starts talking about what happened once she left. She decided to unload all this madness on Ricky but needed a drink first. She tells Ricky, "I'll go to the liquor store since you can't keep your mouth shut!" She giggled. Ricky fired back, "Those punk motherfuckers better leave my girl alone!" "Relax. They weren't bothering me, they hadn't even touched me, but they can look all they want!" Ricky gave her $40 for some liquor. Quianna left and, as she struts toward the store, she passes by the guys. She saw Toddy still sitting in his car staring at her, so she walked past the store and over to him. She said, "Hey, what you been up to?" Dodging her question, Toddy asked, "You still with that chump?"

Quianna was shocked at his attitude and that he had responded that way. She immediately got defensive, "He ain't no chump! I told you! That's my family. What's your problem?"

"You're my problem. You're with him and you supposed to be with me." Quianna was pissed and started walking away, "You know what, I'll check you out when you get your attitude together. I don't even know you!" "Look, if it's like that, y'all can get out of my spot!" Quianna turned around, "Get out your spot?! Hold up, I paid for it! We just used your name. Matter fact...you know what?

Here let's go to the office. We can make this happen now!" Toddy sped off to the hotel but Quianna was on foot. She ran to the room to tell Ricky what was happening and asked him to put the room in his name. Ricky rushed down the steps and went to the office with Quianna trailing behind him. Toddy and Ricky both stared each other down. Quianna stood between them at the counter as the name change took place.

When Toddy left the office, he waited by his car for them to exit. Ricky noticed the guys from the liquor store were watching the whole ordeal play out. He looked at Toddy, "Yo man, what's your problem? Why'd you upset her? I mean, thank you for looking out for her but I got it from here. All that was unnecessary." Toddy, not expecting that reaction, was ready for a fight but didn't get it. Quianna was also surprised and turned on by Ricky's response. Toddy got in his car still angry and upset. He pulled out of the parking lot fast, screeching his wheels. Ricky laughed at the pettiness and asked Quianna, "Wooo, what you do to that brother?" They both laughed and got their liquor from the store. She hugged Ricky and kissed him on his lips as they walked back to the room. They began to drink and the more she drank, the more Quianna talked and cried. She told Ricky everything from beginning to the end.

"So, how'd you get away?"

"I killed him! I slit the bastard's throat. I didn't want to, but I had to get away. It was the only way. Can you believe my mother sold me?"

"Nah, I really can't believe that!"

"Yeah, well. I wouldn't have believed it either, but I saw the texts myself."

"Damn, Key! You killed him? They're going to be looking for you."

"No, they won't. The housekeeper doesn't know my full name and I was kidnapped. They aren't gonna tell on me. But by now, Quinn might be looking for me."

"Hold up, so who's Quinn again?" She stared at the floor, "My bodyguard. He's nothing but a glorified pimp. Always shoving guns in my face, beating us, withholding food, threatening to hurt our families. I hate those people! I swear I'd kill them all, even my mother!" Ricky wrapped his arm around her, "Key, I'm not gonna let nobody hurt you anymore. I promise you that. I'm gonna buy a piece for our protection." She looked up at the popcorn ceiling, laid back on the pink and green flower-covered comforter, and fell asleep.

In the Trauma ICU, Kat was wide awake and cognitive. The doctors gave her a series of exams to see what she knew. She did well but there was no contact person who could verify if the information was correct. One nurse saw Tootie's name in her chart as her contact. *Lucretia Whealer*, Tootie's legal name. The nurse called Tootie, who was at Chan's house, to ask questions confirming the information Kat gave them, all checked out except for her husband. Tootie told the nurse, "She's not married, and she has her address wrong. I'm not sure why she gave an address in Puerto Rico." Chan just sat on the couch listening quietly. The nurse thanked Tootie for the information.

She left Chan's to go back to the hotel. Tomorrow she would be able to move back into her apartment, so she had some packing to get done. When Tootie arrived at the hotel, she called Jean to tell her that Kat was in the hospital. Jean asked, "Oh wow...what's wrong with her?" "She was beat up really bad. She's been in there for a week and a half now. I just couldn't recognize her at first. She's in the Trauma ICU and keeps asking them to call her husband?"

"Oh really?" Jean sounded unsympathetic which was not expected from her best friend and lookout. But after what Jean experienced, she hated Kat and that bastard Eric Morales. She hoped he'd never find her! Tootie interrupted Jean's thoughts, "Where you headed? Sounds like you're in your car." "Oh yeah. I had to go shopping." "Okay, well I'll see you tomorrow then. I'll be back home." Jean answered, "Okay," and hung up. Jean couldn't tell her that she was driving Te'nah to her family in Pennsauken.

At the 'Bricks', Sosa contacted Eric Morales. "Jefe, the young girl isn't around. I went to the apartment the day you sent me. I've been to the parks and I even sat outside her school and her friend's house. I can't find her."

"Are you sure you know what she looks like?" Sosa answered, "Claro, I see her everyday while we're working on the apartment." "Hmm. Her mother must have sent her away. Where's her mother?" Sosa didn't know. "Keep looking. If you find her, bring her to me." Sosa replied, "Esta bien." Morales added, "If you see the mother, bring her to me too." "Okay Bizzi, okay!"

In all the chaos, Jean forgot that she had to go for training with Bett at Tony's bodega, but she had to get her daughter out of harm's way. So she called Bett to let her that know she wouldn't make it to help out at Mr. Tony's store. Jean would do anything for Mr. Tony, they've been good friends for many, many years but Te'nah's safety was priority.

Back at the hospital, Kat was up, moving slowly but able to wash herself. They cleared her to leave Trauma ICU and go to a regular room. She requested something to write on so she could try to figure out her husband's number. After a while, she finally got it and called him. "Hello?" Kat said, "Hello!" Eric stood up from his chair and asked, "Babe, is that you?" "Yes, I'm in the hospital!"

"Where? Tell me. I'm coming for you! Tell me what happened?"

"I was beaten like a dog by my tenant's boyfriend! He beat me bad baby. My face is all messed up. My eyesight is blurry in my left eye and my mouth hurts. I think I'm missing some teeth." Morales was hysterical at the thought that he was powerless and couldn't protect his wife. He's fuming, "Lo mato, te juro que lo mato! (I will kill him, I swear I'll kill him!)" He tells Kat, "Mi amor, just relax. I'm coming now. What hospital baby?" His tone is filled with anger as he continued, "Be calm baby. Papi's coming for you. Get the nurse, mami. I want to speak with her." Kat pressed the call button, and the nurse came in right away and gave him the information he needed. He grabbed his blazer, called his men and headed for the hospital.

Chapter 20

Quianna & Ricky's Plan

"Good morning!" Ricky greeted Quianna with a smile as she opened her eyes, draped in the sheets, covering her from last night's escapades. She smiled back and closed her eyes, her head pounding from an unforgiving hangover.

Ricky stepped onto the balcony that overlooked the main street with his baggie sweatpants, barefoot, and no shirt. He leaned on the railing to call his brother and give him a quick update.

In Newark, Ronnie had been holding the streets down since Ricky left to get Quianna, which was a double win because now they were getting that reward money. Ms. Kat had been gone so it was a good time to show her they could handle the business all by themselves. Every street corner that they owned was doing well since they left the 'Bricks'. They even thought this was a test to see how they would flow without her on the scene.

Ronnie answered the phone, "What's up player? How's Key doing?" "She's good...." Ricky stopped talking as he sees Toddy rolling slow and looking directly at him. "Yo these niggas out here is on some dumb shit. I ain't got no piece and I'm by myself, Ronnie." "Yo, I can be there. I'll book a flight right now and I'm there. Say the word."

"Nawh, I'm gonna lay low until I can get me something." Toddy rolled back, on the other side of the street and pointed at him with smoking gun fingers. This made Ricky nervous. He goes back inside to finish his conversation. Quianna had gone back to sleep. Ricky asked his brother how business was doing. Ronnie gave him good reports on all the corners. Ricky finished talking and hung up with his brother. But he couldn't get Toddy's image out of his mind, Ricky was definitely scared since he wasn't on his turf. Quianna woke up, "Hey, handsome!" "Hey," Ricky had a concerned look on his face.

"What's wrong?"

"Nothing. Just talked to Ronnie, checking on things back home. Ms. Kat hasn't been around. We were running shit." He goes to the window and pulled the curtain back slowly to see if Toddy was still out there. Then walked back towards Quianna.

Ricky grabbed her hands, "It's going to be alright Key. You got me. I ain't going nowhere. But we are gonna have to go back to Jersey. I can't stay out here. I have a business I have to run. And...oh yeah I almost forgot," he threw her I.D. on the bed.

"Where'd you get a picture of me from?"

"Don't worry about it get dressed. We're getting out of here. Pack your bags we'll call a taxi and go to another hotel, maybe Long Beach." She hopped in the shower, changed, and gathered her things. Everything was loaded into the suitcase. Ricky said, "Listen, we'll get a place to stay then we'll go celebrate your birthday. How about it?" Ricky looked up hotels in Long Beach, booked a suite and then called an uber to take the thirty-five-minute ride to Long Beach, California.

Ride to Pennsauken, NJ

Jean and Te'nah took the one-and-a-half-hour trip from Newark to Pennsauken, N.J. On the ride there, Jean explained everything to Te'nah as they are heading down the turnpike. She started explaining how she was the lookout for Kat's drug dealing operation on the street and she was paid $300 a week which put cash in her pocket since she was on section 8 and welfare. "The other day Ms. Kat went missing. No one could find her. I was worried, so I called her husband." Te'nah was stunned, "What? Husband?" "Yes, she has a husband. But no one knows about him. Anyhow those men you called the police on…those are her husband's bodyguards who were coming to look for her. I called her husband to see if he knew where she was, and he didn't know. Then things started falling apart on his end, so he asked me to go to New York, and I did. I helped him find the men you got locked up and we looked for Kat, calling hospitals, jails, everywhere. But everything turned. He tried to have his way with me, and I told him no. Kat and I were friends. But then he said he was going to take you instead just like he did the other girls. I just couldn't...."

"So, he took the girls too? Wait...so Ms. Kat knew her husband took Sheeka and them?"

"I honestly don't know all of that. All I know is that he said it and he said he was coming after you next. And I couldn't have that."

"So mom, what does her husband have to do with Rico?"

"Huh? Rico?"

"Okay, I'll tell you what I know. I saw Nia, Sheeka and Quianna talking to Rico and these guys in a dark blue van. Then they went missing. I wasn't sure if it was Mr. Tony's nephew Rico. I don't go in that store much since he been here, but I went in there to get a better look at him and it was him mom. He was with the girls! Mr. Boots was calling him out too. I should've said something, but I was scared."

"It's okay, sweetie, just don't tell anyone where you are. Not even monster."

"But mom, Ms. Kat had to have known. And why isn't she with her husband? How come nobody knows about him?"

"He's a big drug lord in Puerto Rico. I guess he wanted her to be on the down low over here. Maybe he had her stay in the Bricks so it would look like she doesn't have money, but you know she's a drug lord too. She got everything hemmed up around there. All the drug dealers around there are hers. Nobody even messes with her over there. Eric Morales must have these streets on lock. The police don't even bother her. Kat got everybody slinging dope like crazy. You see how these people are walking around out there. I'm going to be honest with you, I think she was just putting money in my pocket. Sometimes them fiends would get too close and I'd have to run them away from the stoop."

"Mom so you don't think they will hurt you?" Jean answered nervously, "I did think about that. Maybe I will send for my stuff or I'll go back when it gets dark, grab my things and come back down to Pennsauken." As they reached the airport circle they hit a red light and a giant jumbotron on the right flashed Rico's face; *most wanted Newark, NJ resident wanted on sex trafficking minors.* Their mouths dropped!

Jean yelled, "Oh shit! This is for real! I'm done. This shit is too much for me." Jean started crying. "Mom, why are you crying?" "Te'nah, he told me he was coming for you, so I let him have me to save you! But he raped me and said that wasn't good enough! He's still coming for you!"

"Mom, listen, I don't think it's safe for you to go back. They might hurt you."

"I know. You're right. I'm so scared," Jean kept driving trying hard to focus on the road and their next steps.

Eric Morales sees Kat

Mr. Morales showed up at the front desk of Saint Mary's Hospital. "I'm looking for my wife Kathleen Harris Morales." The desk clerk replied, "I'm sorry, sir. We don't have anyone by that name. But let me check Kathleen Harris. Oh yes, here she is." Handing him a visitor's pass, she continues to give him instructions, "Down the hall to our elevators. Then, go to the third floor, sir. Room 309. Morales made his way to her room. As soon as he entered, he pulled back the curtain hastily and it was another female patient who was very heavily sedated. He moved to the next curtain and found his wife's face deformed and bruised. She wasn't the lovely sunset toned queen he fell in love with some years ago. Before, she had to have plastic surgery when he rescued her out of the arms of Jamaican drug lord, Black Bear, who used her as his punching bag. Now she looked like what he remembered after Bear's last beating on her. He was in shock seeing her this way. When he walked in, she was sleeping; and he didn't want to disturb her as he fought back the tears, unconvinced this wasn't retaliation for taking Bear's princess six years ago. Kat opened her eyes to see Morales and his driver standing over her. Mr. Morales addressed his driver, "You can wait in the car. I'll call you to meet me when I'm ready to leave." A soft, sweet tone came from Kat, "Hey baby." He bent down to kiss her swollen lips. Kat moaned in pain. Hearing her groan, he suddenly transformed into this powerless ball of mush, wrapping his arms around her and toppled across her torso crying like a baby. Moments later he came back to himself. "Mamí, I'm sorry I wasn't there to protect you. But I swear to you I will kill him dead, where is he? I will send my guys to take him out now! I promise you that I won't let no one hurt you ever again! You won't leave my side." "It's not your fault papí. Just get his ass and get me out of this hospital. I want to come home with you and lay in your arms. I'm sick of being here."

"Okay, mi amor, but first, tell me everything."

Trip to Long Beach

The Uber pulled up in front of the hotel and Ricky was uneasy, watching his surroundings as they walked down the steps from the upper level. He kept his eyes peeled looking for Toddy and the liquor store boys. Once they were in the car heading for Long Beach, he let out a sigh of relief. He hugged his girl and pulled her close for a kiss. "Happy birthday, baby. We're on our way now," he looked around one more time before they hit the CA/110 highway. Quianna noticed his unease, "You okay? You look like something got your mind." "Nah, I'm good, don't you worry your pretty little head." "Umm, is it about back home?" "Yeah, we gotta head back soon," he deflected, but clearly worried about Toddy and his boys.

When they arrived, they checked into The Residence Inn Long Beach Downtown. Quianna was taken aback by the hotel's features. The lobby was spacious and beautifully decorated, the outdoor patio had a huge fireplace and lounge area, and the view of the Pacific Ocean from the pool was unlike anything she had ever seen. She was ecstatic and felt safe for the first time since she left the 'Bricks'. She suggested they check out more of the hotel. Ricky had booked it for three days for a total of about $600. Quianna listened in on Ricky and the desk receptionist's conversation, "Are you sure you can afford that?" "Girl you know how I roll." They laughed as he confidently placed his hand on the small of her back. They head to the roof lounge and ordered drinks, relaxing on the big lounge chairs. "You're my girl, nothing is too much for you." She giggled as she tells him, "Oh so…you just gonna make me your girl?"

"Yeah…I am. It's me and you, Key. You know. We don't have to go back to Newark, but I do have to get back to my business. Maybe we can get a place in Irvington?"

Out of nowhere, her mind raced back to killing Armon in the pool. She choked and spit out her drink. "What's wrong? Yo, you okay?" She held her hand out for him to grab. He instantly held her hand, crawled over to the chaise with her, and repeated the question as he wrapped his arms around her. "I - I just keep seeing his face. The guy I killed," she whispered in his ear. "Hey…he

deserved it. Don't let it get to you. You can't."
"But how…you ever kill anybody?"

"Yeah…these two fiends kept bugging me to get them high. They tried to threaten me with the police. The one guy tried to come at me with a knife and I was pissed so I killed his ass. I had to!"

"Well I'm not like that, Ricky. I'm not like you. I had a nightmare last night."

"I know you're not. It will be alright Key, I promise."

He got up to look at the view over the roof top, gazing down on the street he noticed a Black BMW with chrome rims circling the hotel. Ricky couldn't believe his eyes and thought, 'This guy couldn't have followed us to Long Beach! Oh my God, what am I gonna do?' He followed the car with his eyes as it turned at the light. He hurried around the roof top edge to get a better look. "What are you looking at," Quianna asked, relaxing on the lounge chaise with her feet crossed and arms folded behind her head but wondering why Ricky was acting so strange. "Nothing, it's nothing," he replied, "I was just checking out the scenery." He sat back down to avoid any more suspicion. Then, he changed the subject, "Are you enjoying your birthday?"

"Yes, I am! Thank you! Thank you for coming to take care of me. Honestly, it feels so nice to know someone cares and I'm not alone. I've been through a lot," she put her head down reflecting on the last few months. Ricky lifted her head with one finger and looked into her eyes. "You don't have to worry anymore. I told you I'm never leaving you again."

Ricky and Quianna relaxed on the rooftop for almost an hour, but Ricky was uneasy about the thought of being followed by Toddy. He shot back up, "Come on, let's go to the pool and enjoy your birthday, alright!" "Ricky don't you miss your brother?" she asked unexpectedly. "Yeah, I do. I definitely wanna get back home before Ms. Kat gets back, they say she's been missing. She's been gone before I left to come out here. Wait til she sees how we've been handling our business. It almost feels like it's a test to see how we'd do."

"Oh wow! Ms. Kat ain't no joke. She be keeping them fiends in check. I remember one time I was going in the house from karate and this drugged out white guy wouldn't let me up the steps. Ms. Kat pushed me behind her and hit him with this bat in his knees so hard, ha. I was surprised she stood up for me." Ricky laughed, "Yeah, she's no joke. I think she probably went to see her husband."

"Her husband?"

"Oh! You can't tell nobody!"

"Come on Ricky. Be for real! After all I went through? And what I've done? I'm not saying shit!" Ricky divulged that her husband is a big King Pin in Puerto Rico who also fools with sex trafficking. Quianna's eyes widened as she listened to Ricky and she jumped up, "Hold up, you don't think he had anything to do with me being trafficked do you?" Disgusted, she continued, "Did Ms. Kat know Rico?" "No, she didn't even like him. He would try to talk to her, and she would just ignore him."

Quianna's voice got louder, "What if she knew him and didn't want anyone else to know she knew him. What if her husband knew Rico or he worked for him?"

"I didn't see signs of that. But it's not impossible." Quianna looked away, wondering if it could be possible. "I don't think she would do that to me or my mom, but can you really trust someone who sells drugs to people and ruins their lives only so they can get rich?" "Hey!," Ricky interjected taking control of the conversation, "It's your birthday! Enough of that! Let's go." They headed to the elevator passing by a housekeeper who looked at Quianna and said, "Oh you must be Mrs.

Lee's daughter? You look just like you mother!"
Surprised by the remark, Quianna answered, "No,
I'm sorry, I'm from Jersey you have me mistaken
for someone else." The housekeeper was
embarrassed, "Oh I'm so sorry!" Quianna smiled
back, "No problem!" They got off on their floor
and passed a maintenance man. "You look just
like your mom!" The maintenance man came
down from the ladder.

Quianna laughed, "You're the second one to say
something to me. Mrs. Lee, right?" "Yeah."
Quianna replied, "I'm not her daughter. Where
does this Mrs. Lee work anyway?"

"She's the manager here."

"Oh! Well, I'd like to see her since I'm assuming
she can be my twin!"

"If you want to, you can find her at the front desk."

They entered the room to change into their
swimsuits. The maintenance man went to the front
desk to tell Mrs. Lee there was someone in the
hotel she had to meet, "She's a spitting image of
you, I'm telling you! But she's young. Very
young." Mrs. Lee was curious and asked what
room. "Room 224. She really looks like you!" He
walked off and Mrs. Lee quickly thought of her
child who was kidnapped almost eighteen years

ago. She's always looking at faces hoping that one day she'd bump into her and find her.

The television was on while they changed, and before they could turn it off to leave the room breaking news came on of the Famous Vitner, Armon Vazquell, found dead in an LA County Homicide Investigation. "That's him! Oh my God! That's the man I killed! They must have found him!" She watched the segment with a blank stare on her face but not much of a reaction about the death. "Let's go to the pool," she walked out, her mind still marinating on the fact that Ms. Kat might have been involved with the girls' kidnapping. Though she wasn't positive, the possibility was floating in her head. Ricky simply stared at her, this definitely wasn't the same girl that he knew.

Rico and Larry stop in Maryland

Larry and Rico stopped at a motel in Maryland to rest and gather their thoughts after their explosive day. The motel was low budget and dingy. They pulled up to loud music and girls hanging over the rails surrounded by a cloud of smoke and laughter. To the left were some guys cleaning their cars with forty ounce beers on the walkway. Larry and Rico were amazed at the prospects in this place. They sent the girls to their rooms in pairs. Rico and Larry shared one. The girls were instructed not to leave their rooms. Since the people at the motel seemed to be coupled up, they didn't want any unwarranted attention or problems.

After Larry and Rico had a round with the girls at the bar next to the motel, they headed to the car to check out any prospects. It was late and the only thing shining was the moon. Even the dimly lit parking lot lights added to the darkness. There was no way a passerby would check into this motel for fear of being robbed while trying to get into their room. The motel clerk could see all the activity on camera but would never call the police, it would be bad for business. You could tell the kind of low-class environment this was, anything goes at this place. The guys called it a night and headed for the room.

Chapter 21

Sheeka Misses Her Flight

Agent Daniels and Sheeka were still in Atlanta, sitting together in the conference room and she tells Sheeka, "We're going to get you something to eat. Your flight is tonight and there will be a female agent accompanying you home to meet your family." Sheeka was trying to focus on what Daniels was saying, but she needed a fix. She starts sweating and her stomach begins to hurt. She's getting more and more agitated with every word. Sheeka blurted out, "I think…I'm getting sick." She hurried over to the trash but missed the mark and threw up on the floor inches away. Her stomach started to knot up and she laid curled up on the floor, moaning. She had gone two hours without a fix, and she was feeling it.

Daniels immediately called for an ambulance for Sheeka. She was taken to the local hospital to be treated and Daniels went with her to make sure she got faster treatment since her flight was in a couple of hours. But Sheeka was not given anything and instead was released. She was sent back to the station and Agent Daniels was told that they couldn't just give out methadone even in her withdrawal. Typically patients are signed up in advance to receive it from a Methadone Clinic. There was nothing they could do. Daniels had to send Sheeka home sick and withdrawing on the plane. But she was in no shape to fly. So her flight home was postponed until she could get her composure together. Agent Daniels called Sheeka's mom to inform her that she would not be returning home on the night flight. Her return status is on hold, pending the status of her recovery.

On the phone, Vivian was quite upset, "What you mean she's not coming home?"

"Ma'am, I'm sorry but Sheeka is very sick right now. She is in the withdrawal process and it's better that she goes through it here with professionals that can help her through it rather than her withdrawing at home. She's going to need treatment because her brain will want the drug. Sheeka has a long road ahead of her and I suggest counseling as well."

Vivian inquired, "Well how bad is she?" "She's vomiting, cramping, and she's been sweating profusely. The process is really bad on an adult, so just imagine how it is for a child."

"This is complete shit!"

"Excuse me ma'am?" Daniels was surprised to hear Vivian's reaction.

"You…heard…me. I said this is shit! I…I raised her the best way…I know how. She was the best of my kids…and now…now because she made a mistake. One mistake! All of us gotta uproot our lives? Or, or…be on alert 'cause this little shit done fucked up? Really? This is some bullshit!"

Daniels cleared her throat, "Ms. Vivian, I'm not sure exactly how your life will turn out because of this tragedy. But can I give you a word of advice?"

Vivian answered with sarcasm, "What's that?"

"Your daughter is alive. I could have been calling you with news that you'd need to make funeral arrangements rather than flight arrangements. Secondly, you might need to put Sheeka first and think about her feelings and all that she's been through. She is only a child and she's been victimized. And she definitely doesn't need you to make her feel guilty. Thirdly…."

"Thirdly what?"

"Thirdly…you should stop drinking and protect your daughter and your other kids!" Vivian hung up on Agent Daniels.

The Vintner Investigation

The officers were at the estate questioning the housekeeper. "Do you know if Mr. Vasquell had any company here last night? Any visitors? Maybe on business matters?"

Sandra answered, "I'm only the housekeeper. I don't get involved in Mr. Vasquell's matters or his business."

"Do you know of anyone who would want to see him dead? Enemies? Business rivals?"

"No, no. I don't know." Sandra looked away from the officer.

"Well, ma'am I understand you're upset, but I suggest you cooperate and tell us everything you know because right now you're our only suspect."

"Me?! Oh Dios mio! (Oh my God) No, no I would never hurt Mr. Armon, never! He was a good boss!"

"Then I suggest you cooperate fully. When was the last time you saw him alive?"

"Monday night. I left to go home once my work was done. He was alive!"

"Okay, and what time was that?" "Six pm. I always leave at six. Was anyone here with him when you left, or did he mention anyone was coming over?" Sandra hesitated. If she told the police about the escort, then she'd uncover the whole prostitution thing. She quickly made eye contact with the officer, "No, he never mentioned anyone coming over. He would only do that if I was here and the guests were invited." "Okay, well, did he have an appointment book or calendar?"

Before she could answer, Sgt. Mullen arrived and took over questioning Sandra, "Ma'am are there cameras here?" "Yes, but they only face the front of the house...oh and the vineyards. They're not in the house."

"Very well, please show me his office and appointment book. Ma'am, when was the last time he had company?" "He really didn't have much company."

"Was he in a romantic relationship with anyone?"

"Oh no...none that I know."

"Please understand I have to ask this; were you having an affair with him? Romantically involved?"

"What? Absolutely not! No, I wasn't," Sandra was disgusted at the thought.

The officer chimed in, as a woman's underwear hung from his pencil, "Well somebody was definitely here. I found these under his bed. But you said he didn't have much company, or he'd have them when you were around. So, either these are yours or you're a horrible housekeeper. Or both?"

Now Sandra was scared and nervous. She had to give them something because things weren't looking good for her. The surveillance tape shows a town car enter the gate. Five days prior there was also a delivery truck that entered the gate and left. They also saw Sandra coming and going from the estate every day. "Who is the person in the delivery truck?"

"I believe it's a company who picks up the wine." The officer asked, "So they come to the house?" "No. Not normally but I think they were picking up a check."

"Okay. Who's in the town car?" Sandra cleared her throat before answering, "Umm, I'm not sure." The officer was getting impatient, "Listen. You need to think because it's not looking too good for you! You lied about Mr. Vasquell receiving guests, and you're hiding something now!" Sandra nervously replied, "Okay. Mr. Vasquell sometimes has ladies over to entertain him…if you know what I mean."

Mr. Tony's Bodega

At the store, Bett showed up early for training with Mr. Tony. She noticed the screen door was unlocked so she walked in slowly and called Mr. Tony's name. But there was no answer. She called his name out again as she reached the counter. She looked around the store and turned her head slightly over the counter, discovering Mr. Tony's body lying in a pool of blood! Bett screamed in horror and backed away, running into the potato chip rack behind her and knocking it down. She fell to the floor screaming at the top of her lungs. Realizing what she had seen, she ran through the door and into a fiend knocking him over into the street. She kept running, hollering for Mr. Willie, nearly getting hit by a car. Boots heard the car horn and Bett's screams, so he hurried to the end of the building to see what was wrong.

"Bett! What's wrong?" Bett was banging on Mr. Willie's door with such urgency and intensity, that he grabbed her from behind and turned her around.

"Hey! I said, what's wrong?"

"Mr. Tony! Mr. Tony! He's dead! Somebody killed him!" crying in his arms. Mr. Willie came to the door looking surprised, Boots immediately told him about Mr. Tony. "Call the police!" Reverend Briggs pulled up to open the church for prayer. He can see the hysteria, "What's happening here Boots?" Tony's over there, dead at the store! Someone killed him! Bett just found him!" Bett was still crying uncontrollably. Rev. Briggs screamed, "Oh my God, Lord help us! Has anyone called the police?" "I just told Willie. He's calling right now!" Rev. Briggs said, "Has anyone checked to see if he's alive?" Boots shook his head. Mr. Willie came back from informing the NPD of the incident. They told him someone had already called, and the police were on their way. Ten minutes had passed and with the news of Mr. Tony's death, people ran in to loot the place, some with cartons of cigarettes and lottery tickets. Boots yelled for them to leave as he held Bett to comfort her. Still, the cash register was robbed as one fiend stepped over Mr. Tony's lifeless body. But once the police arrived, the people scattered.

The police took control of the scene, taping everything off, and started their investigation. Tony had been lying on the floor all night, no one even paid attention to the security gate which wasn't pulled down last night. He closed his store on time for 20 years. He had never been robbed and always looked out for the community. He was the town watch president and city council member. Hours passed by and it was a brisk 50 degrees outside as the people hung from their windowsills watching their friend and confidant get rolled out covered in a hard, plastic bag on a stretcher. The bodega had been their local grocery store for those who couldn't make it to the big supermarkets. Bett never stopped crying as she saw him being rolled away. Mr. Willie shed a tear with his head down, turned around and went back in his house.

The NPD questioned everyone from the delivery trucks that pulled up to neighbors and spectators. Hours went by and no one had seen anything. The police locked up Tony's Bodega, sealed the entrance with yellow tape, and left. Around the block, the mood was somber as neighbors stood around in shock. Two detectives stayed behind talking outside of the bodega. Rev. Briggs started crying for his friend whom he'd known for over 20 years, "He was an honest, a well-rounded person everyone respected. All these years living here. How could someone kill him? He was a good man."

Rev. Briggs walked over to speak with the detectives. He described Mr. Tony as a pillar in the community. He told them Mr. Tony had no family members there, other than a nephew who came to live with him and who could possibly be connected to the abduction of the 3 little girls as he pointed to the brownstone. The detective asked, "Where's the nephew now?" Rev. Briggs informed him that he hadn't seen him since the kidnapping. The detective asked if the young lady who found him was around. Briggs called Bett over, who is visibly shaken. Bett spoke with the detectives. The police were gone but the streets were left with a sense of loss and despair and the brick building with a large red awning that read "TONY'S BODEGA".

It was like a curse had run over the streets and it all started with Mr. Tony's decision to help his sister's son, but a lot of people got hurt in the process. Rico's arrival had caused a lot of havoc around him and now Mr. Tony was dead! The street was silent, no one knew how to move on from here. Rev. Briggs grabbed hold of Bett to comfort her. "It's okay baby, it's okay," he rocked her back and forth. Suddenly, she pulled away without saying anything and headed for the steps of the 'Bricks'.

Tootie's Secret

Tootie was called down to Human Resources. 'Maybe my luck had finally run out,' she thought as she went to the HR office. "Hi. I was called down, you wanted to see me?" The HR Supervisor answered, "Yes, Detective Stevens is here to ask you some questions. When he's done, we'd like to ask you some questions ourselves." Unsure of her next move, her mind went straight to an exit door. She thought she was going there to sign papers for the family leave she had requested because her daughter was missing. But now she was blindsided by the detective's presence at her job. The detective looked narrowly into her eyes, as if there was something he knew. Sweat starts forming on her upper lip and in the palms of hands. She says to herself, 'Think fast Tootie, think fast!'

Her HR Supervisor said, "I'm going to bring you into the conference room where you can have some privacy and, Lucretia, when you're finished, please come into my office. I will make sure that your shift is covered until this interview is over." The supervisor ushered them to the conference room and shut the door. Detective Stevens looked down at some documents in his hand and addressed her, "Ms. Whealer, we're here because of a missing child's case from 18 years ago at Long Beach Hospital in California. You were a maternity nurse there, is that right?" "Yes, that is correct. What's going on, detective? Are they re-opening the case? Because…I've already been interviewed about this case and I told them everything I knew. Why are you coming to my job? Why couldn't you contact me at home or something? This isn't a good look coming to my job."

Before Detective Stevens could answer, she interrupted, "Listen, I came down here without going to the bathroom. My bladder is about to bust! I can't hold it! Excuse me while I go to the bathroom and I'll come right back and answer anything you want." Det. Stevens was confused but agreed to let her go, "Oh, okay. No problem. Go ahead and come right back." Shaking her head yes, Tootie thought to herself, 'Okay! Smart Tootie!' She left the bathroom and walked back past the conference room making sure the detective was still reviewing the papers in his hand, she went through the automatic doors to the parking lot. Then she ran to her car and drove away. As Tootie's driving, she grabbed her phone and called Chan.

"Hey pretty lady!"

Tootie replied, "Listen. I don't have time right now, I need your help! This detective is at my job. I made a run for it, help me!" Chan replied, "Drive here, put your car in my garage and stay here for a couple of days until I can get you away from here."

"Ok, I'm on my way."

It had been longer than five minutes and Detective Stevens went to the HR Supervisor's office, "Excuse me, Ms. Whealer went to the bathroom a while ago and hasn't returned. Can you please check the bathrooms to make sure she's alright?" The HR supervisor went into the bathroom and it was empty. She came out and said, "I'm sorry, but she's not here. Let's go back into the conference room to see if she went back. Maybe we just missed her." They walked back but Tootie wasn't there. The supervisor said, "Hmm…I'll check her floor to see if she went back there. It will only take a moment." She picked up the phone, asked the desk nurse for Tootie, then hung up. "I'm so sorry, detective. She's not on her floor."

A look of disapproval on his face, Stevens replied, "I'll go back to the conference room and make a few phone calls from there in case she shows up. But if she doesn't, I'll let you know what happens from there." The HR supervisor walked through the hospital trying to find her employee as she had just learned that Tootie could be the child abductor at Long Beach Hospital 18 years ago.

Chapter 22

Sheeka Comes Home

Sheeka finally made it to her flight, though it was rough and she was irritated and agitated, she still made it! She complained about muscle cramps and was up and down all throughout her flight. They landed in a few hours and headed to her home. Now Sheeka had been gone for 4 and a 1/2 months and, in those months, had been through a lot – and she looked like it. They arrived at the brownstone and Bett was sitting on the stoop. Sheeka got out of the car and ran over to Bett. They embraced in a long affectionate hug and cried together. Seeing Sheeka again, after witnessing Mr. Tony's body took an emotional toll on Bett. Still she was excited and relieved to see Sheeka. "OMG! Girl! Where have you been?"

The officer butt in, "Excuse me. I have to take you to your mother and it's cold out here. We need to go!" Bett took a long look at Sheeka and said, "Go ahead. Go ahead, I'll see you later." Sheeka let go of Bett and shrugged her shoulders at the agent with an attitude. "Okay. I'll see you later I guess. I'll come up to your apartment." Bett replied, "Okay, get settled with your family and I'll see you later." They proceeded to her mom's apartment and knocked on the door. Her little brother opened the door, took one look at Sheeka, and slammed the door in her face. Sheeka and the agent looked at each other before Vivian opened the door to welcome Sheeka with a hug. Sheeka reluctantly hugged back, not knowing which mother she was going to get. The drunk one or the sober one? Then she quickly realized it was the sober one. Vivian kissed Sheeka all over her face and Sheeka pushed back, "Okay, that's enough! Stop, that's enough! I'm here."

The agent stated, "I'm glad you have your child back alive, ma'am. It was my honor to be able to deliver her to you. She has a long way to go, but she should be alright." "Thank you so much," Vivian kept glancing back at her daughter who had aged considerably. The agent sat for a moment longer with Vivian, explaining their next steps on moving forward having declined witness protection, and then she left. As she moved toward the front door of the building, Bett looked up at the sound of the door opening and asked, "Is she gonna be okay?" The agent sighed, "I sure hope so," and she got into the black SUV. Upstairs, Vivian asked, "So, Sheeka, how are you, honey? They said you weren't feeling well." Her brothers shyly stood by the living room doorway, staring at her. Sheeka noticed and said, "What the hell are ya'll looking at?!" She rushed over and hit one of them in the head. "And why you shut the door in my face?" He started crying. Vivian shouted, "Hey what's wrong with you, Sheeka, don't ever do that again!" She went over to console her son. "Listen, I don't care if he shut the door in your face. You don't put your hands on him!"

"Oh, of course…you taking up for him? Really?! Nobody cares about what happened to me?" She stormed out of the house, slamming the door behind her, and rushed downstairs to the building's front doors to look for Bett. She didn't see her but thought she could use a fix. So, she went to see Boots at his wooden hut on the side of the building. Boots wasn't around. Sheeka turned on the light attached to the extension cord leading to the basement and starts rummaging through his stuff trying to find enough change to buy a bag from Ricky or Ronnie. She reached into his torn box spring and pulled out a roll of money in a rubber band. Her eyes widened but she didn't hesitate to take it and ran out.

Heading down the alley, she bumped into Gary, a bum living in the alley of the building on the next block. Gary knew everybody at the 'Bricks'. "Hey girl, I see your back home! Glad you're okay!" He extended his arms to hug her as she pushes him away. Sheeka, not in the mood for the theatrics, was on a mission to find Ronnie. Gary continued, "Hey, Boots in there? I know he was so happy to see you!"

"I didn't come out of there!"

"Yes, you did I just saw you go in there."

"No! I didn't go in there you white piece a shit!" She walked faster and faster, then jogged away. Gary stood in place watching her, then went into Boots' hut to see why she was in there, finding it a sheer mess. Suddenly, Boots walked in seeing Gary go through his things. "What the hell are you doing in here!" Gary was surprised at Boots' reaction since he had gone in to check his belongings. "Relax. The little girl was in here, so I just came to make sure she didn't take anything." Boots asked, "What the hell you talking about? What little girl?"

"The girl. Ahh…Sheeka, that's her name. Vivian's daughter."

"Are you serious right now? Man, after all we've been through your gonna to lie to me?" Boots knelt down to look for his pan handling money. He begins throwing his stuff around in panic, "Where the hell is my money, Gary?" He rushed at Gary and threw him on the wooden nightstand Sosa made for him. Gary, stunned, fought back. "You didn't take some of my money you took all of it!" Boots kept shouting. Gary regained his composure, "No, I didn't! Let me prove it to you." He held his stomach as he got back up.

Boots pushed him out and they both headed to the front of the building. A light rain starts coming down and they saw Bett looking out her window. Boots motioned for her to come down, so Bett opened the building door slowly. Boots and Gary pushed their way in. "Umm. What's Up?" Bett inquired, feeling uncomfortable about Gary being in the building. Boots yelled, "Bett, is Sheeka home?" Then he turned and gave Gary an evil stare. "Yeah, she got in today...why?" Gary clamored, "See? I told you!" Boots looked at Bett with anger, "My money is missing, and Gary said that he saw her coming out of my spot." They heard loud voices arguing in the back of the building and ran to the back where Sheeka was begging Ronnie for drugs. Ronnie held a large roll of money in his hand that he took from Sheeka. Boots ran over to Ronnie, "Hey boy! That's my money!" Ronnie looked at Sheeka and said, "I got it off Sheeka, she was trying to buy some dope with it." He tossed it to Boots.

Boots looked back at Gary, "I'm sorry man!" Gary shook his head in forgiveness. Then, Boots turned back to Sheeka, "Girl, don't ever steal from me again, you hear me!" Sheeka disputed, "Don't nobody want your shit! Ain't nobody steal from you! You better go 'head!" Bett jumped in, "Really Sheeka?! You just got back, and you stole from Mr. Boots? Really?!" "And she didn't steal a little bit, she stole my whole bag!" Boots continued.

"I told you! I ain't steal shit!" Sheeka kept denying the accusation. But Gary interrupted, "I saw you come out of Boots' hut with my own eyes! It was you! That's why you were in such a hurry."

"I'm gonna punch you right in your face for lying on me you fuckin bum!" Bett got in Sheeka's face and held her arms, "Hey! Hey! What is wrong with you? You straight buggin!" She told Boots, "I'll take care of her! Let me handle this." Sheeka rolled her eyes, "Yeah. Whatever!"

The Infamous Mrs. Lee

In sunny Long Beach, Ricky asked Quianna, "You okay, babe?" "I'm fine. It's my birthday!" Quianna smiled as they walked to the elevator. The elevator doors opened and a brown-skinned tall black lady with a blue dress suit, brown heels, and a hotel logo on her blazer looked directly at Quianna. "Hi!

Quianna, is it? I'm Mrs. Lee, room 224 right?" Quianna paused as they stepped into the elevator, "Uhh...why?" Mrs. Lee continued, "Oh, I'm the manager. I was told I had a twin, and I was just trying to find out if it was you." She laughed. Quianna responded, "Mrs. Lee?" "Yes!"

"Oh okay. Yeah, I wanted to come meet you, I've been stopped twice about being your daughter." They both laughed looking each other over to see if there was any resemblance. "That's funny. But you could be my daughter! You do look like me."

"Do you have any children?"

"Just a son. I did have a daughter...once."

"Once? Did she die?" Ricky mumbled, "Key, don't ask her that!" Mrs. Lee replied, "Oh, it's okay. No, she didn't die. She was kidnapped...18 years ago today, as a matter of fact. Today is her birthday!" Mrs. Lee's expression grew sad.

"Wow, I'm sorry to hear that." Just then elevator doors opened as they arrived on their floor and Quianna said, "Well, pleasure meeting you." Mrs. Lee smiled, "Yes, me too! Call the front desk if you need anything." Ricky responded, "We probably won't be here long. I'm taking Key out for her birthday today." They got off on their floor and the elevator doors closed. Mrs. Lee's heart dropped, immediately tears begin to well up in her eyes. She held onto the elevator railing as it went up. The elevator finally stopped, and more guests got on. Mrs. Lee smiled, quickly trying to compose herself.

Quianna and Ricky swam in the pool for a bit then returned to their room to shower and get dressed for their night out. Ricky searched his phone for a night club to surprise Quianna. But first, dinner at a local restaurant and bar near the hotel. They walked there, kissing and holding hands. 'Umm, I swear I just seen a car that looks just like Toddy's. I must be bugging!' Ricky's heart is pounding as he recalled the same thought earlier when he was on the roof. He squeezed Quianna's hand and begins to walk faster almost pulling her along. "Hey slow down! What's wrong?" Ricky, realizing he was acting awkward, said, "Oh, we're almost there. I'm just excited that we're celebrating your birthday together."

Shortly after arriving, they're seated and place their orders. The music was playing, and people were dancing. Quianna was excited. She felt like a real person, a grown woman; she felt normal for the first time in a long time. She tried to turn up, but she couldn't get the thought of Ms. Kat and her husband's involvement in her kidnapping out of her head. She thought, 'And where's Rico now. Is he out there somewhere trying to traffic other girls?' Her mind was in a deep, dark place and Ricky began to notice. He tried to pull her out of it, "Hey, hey! What are you thinking about? Here I got you a Rum & Coke. Girl, it's your birthday! Get out your head and let's party!" Quianna agreed and spun off the barstool with a drink in one hand and popping her fingers to the music with her other hand.

She danced to Fifty Cents' Lollipop and a few hours had passed by. Staggering out of the bar, holding on to Ricky, they walked as they laughed about the silliest things. He nixed the night club idea and was trying his best to be in control of the situation, but he was just as bad off as Quianna. They made it back to their room and started making out which quickly escalated from there. Just before midnight, Quianna got hungry so they went out again to look for an open spot. They headed to a street behind the hotel. They were walking for a while when they came upon some locals and asked them what was open at that time. They got directions to a little taco spot and kept walking. As they crossed the dark street, car lights ambush them from behind with some speed. They scrambled to get on the sidewalk as the car flew down the street.

Quianna screamed, "What the hell? We almost got ran the over by that ass!" "I don't even think they saw us," Ricky said, catching his breath. They were both shook but continued in the direction of the store. The car drove to the end of the dark street and spun around heading back in their direction. It barreled down the street heading right for them. With no time to move, they saw the car going faster this time. Ricky pushed Quianna out of the way but was hit head on! He flipped over the hood and in the air repeatedly before landing on the ground with a hard thud. Quianna screamed in horror and rushed over to his body as he lied motionless. "Ricky! No! Oh my God!" She cradled his head on her lap while wiping the blood from his face. The black BMW with chrome wheels rode away slowly.

She gasped, "Help somebody! Please! Help!!" The BMW peeled off, burning rubber, and turned back around. Quianna was terrified! She dropped Ricky's head and ran between two buildings down a dark street, leaving Ricky's lifeless body on the ground. Meanwhile, the car sped back up the street aiming at Ricky's body again. If Ricky wasn't taken out the first time, he was damn sure going to be taken out this time. Quianna watched in horror as her friend lost his life right before her eyes. Ricky was the only one who took the time to come save her, the only one who truly loved her for her and now he's gone! When the car was completely out of sight, she ran over to his body and went through his pockets. She took all his money and his cell phone and ran back between the buildings. Shaking and crying as she ran, she slid into the back of a restaurant that was closing for the night and sat in the corner on a damp, sticky floor mat.

The workers were cleaning up for the night and took no notice of her. Pots and pans clinking, you could hear talking and laughter. Quianna watched them as she cried in the corner. She played back in her mind what just happened and realized it was Toddy! And that he wasn't just after Ricky, he was after her too! She pulled her knees to her chest wondering, if he would find her and try to quiet her should she walk out the door. Then she put her head down on her knees.

Te'nah's Secret Conversation

Te'nah called Monster and he answered, "What up girl? I miss you. Where you at?" "I can't say, I promised my mom I wouldn't say." Monster pressed, "Come on girl, you know I won't say nothing!" "I know. What ya'll been doing? Are you back at the Bricks?" Monster gave her the run

246

down, "Yea, we been back. Ms. Kat is missing. This place don't seem the same. Sheeka is back, all messed up. She stole Mr. Boot's money! He beat up his boy, Gary, thinking he took it, but then Bett let her in our house so Mr. Boots wouldn't jack her up and she stole Bett's earrings my mom got her last Christmas. Crazy!"

"Damn! That's messed up. So, what you mean Ms. Kat still missing? Dang, that's been a long time!" Monster replied, "Yeah. It has. I got to get work though. I'm about to see if Rev. Briggs will let me do some work around the church and…oh My God! I almost forgot to tell you! They found Mr. Tony shot dead in his store!" Te'nah couldn't believe what she just heard, "What?! Oh My God!" She starts to cry, "Everything is going wrong. What happened? Who did it? When is his funeral?"

"I don't know. His store is closed. Bett found him and she's really messed up about the whole thing."

"That's so horrible," she paused, "So, why you need money?" Monster explained, "I have to buy some new clothes. I have a college tour and I want to look nice. I need like $500 for a new wardrobe and my moms can't really afford it. You know."

"Oh…well, I can give you $100. I'm really proud of you. You came a long way Monster. You don't have to give me the money back."

"Where you get $100 from?"

"My dad. I'll send it out today but I'm gonna have to put my address on there. Please promise me you won't tell anyone. Promise me! My mom will kill me!" Monster continued his interrogation, "What's the secret? Where you at?"

"Look, I can't tell you now, just don't tell anyone. Not even your mom!" Monster backed off, "Okay, okay! Thanks Nae." Te'nah went back to the sad news, "Damn, Mr. Tony! Do they know who killed him?"

"No, they don't. They're still investigating. But listen, there's someone at the door, I'll call you back." She replied, "Okay, I'll call you later!"

Chapter 23

Quianna was tucked away in the restaurant's storage area all night long. Since she was a small 130 lbs., she was able to hide without being seen. She had all night to think, trying to wrap her head around what just happened. Once again, she's alone. Morning came and the doors to the restaurant were opened. She woke up to the loud conversations of the workers. She scurried out the back door to the bright light of the California sun. She was nervous about seeing Ricky's body again. She went through the buildings' walkway and saw police, ambulances, and crime tape where she had left Ricky, so she turned around in the opposite direction towards her hotel. As she entered her hotel, Quianna was greeted by the smiling faces of the front desk staff. The door opened and Mrs. Lee walked out to greet her all chipper and happy to see her, "Good morning!" Her face quickly changed seeing Quianna's hair and clothes disheveled. She asked Quianna, "Are you okay?" Quianna answered, "No," and started crying. Mrs. Lee hugged her and said, "Come on. Let's get you to your room." Quianna cried harder, "I…don't…have my key,"

Mrs. Lee told her not to worry and asked the front desk clerk for a key to Room 224. Quianna lifted her head, "How'd you know what room I was in?" She had forgotten the conversation they had just yesterday in the elevator with Ricky. Mrs. Lee replied, "Girl, I know everything around here. I'm the manager!" She smiled and tapped her on the arm. The smell of fresh coffee filled the air and Mrs. Lee asked, "Hey. Are you hungry?" Quianna was starving, "Yes!" "Well, okay, let's have breakfast then." They walked to the breakfast area and Mrs. Lee mentioned, "You seem a bit shaken. Are you okay? Where's your friend?" Quianna thought up a quick lie, "Umm, I can't find him. We got separated. I came back here to see if he was here. I'll eat a bite with you but then I have to go up to the room to see if he's there." In her heart, she thought, she'll never see her friend again because he was dead on the streets of Long Beach and he was only there because of her.

Mrs. Lee studied Quianna's face, "Wow. You really do look like me, I can see it. You have eyes like mine." Quianna looked at her, "You mentioned your daughter was kidnapped. Did they ever find her?"

"No, never. But I still pray that I'll find her someday." Quianna begins to cry. "What's wrong?

It's okay, I didn't mean to get you upset. Are you okay?"

"I'm sorry, it's just so sad." She couldn't control her emotions, as she visualized the police tape the reality about Ricky set in. Mrs. Lee's story about her daughter was her opportunity to cry. Quianna apologized, wiping her tears. Mrs. Lee repeated herself, "Are you sure you're okay? You're not eating and you're playing with your food." Angrily, Quianna lifted her head quickly, "I'm fine!" Her emotions shifted sporadically, and Mrs. Lee apologized for pressing the issue. Quianna pushed back from the table and threw her napkin on her plate, "I have to go to my room." She grabbed the room key off the table and put it in her purse draped across her shoulder and headed to her room. Mrs. Lee was speechless, she didn't think she had done or said anything to warrant that type of response.

Quianna speed-walked to her room and once inside she fell flat on the bed crying her eyes out. She looked up for a moment and found the handwritten letter from Ricky on the bed. She opened the envelope that was addressed: *To the Birthday Girl*. And read the card quietly.

'Key, I have always had a crush on you. I've always wanted you to be my girl and now that I

have you, I'm never gonna let you go! You got me for life and I'm 100% sure you'll have me, I want you to be my wife. I promise, I'll never leave you! I'll always protect you. Keep this chain around your neck. And I have the other one, and we will be inseparable. Me and you forever! Love ya Baby, Happy Birthday!'

She sobbed feverishly and threw the card across the room. "Why?!! Why is everything happening to me? God help me! God you said if I called on you, you'd answer me…I've been calling on you!! So please answer me! Why is all this happening to me?" She snatched her purse and pulled out Ricky's phone to call Boots. After a few rings, he answered, "Hello?" "Hi Mr. Boots" she said through her tears.

"Baby girl?"

"Yes."

"What's wrong Baby?" Quianna exclaimed, "Everything! Everything is wrong! I just can't handle all this! I miss my mom, this world is so scary. I just needed to hear your voice. You always calmed me down." Boots exhaled, "Come home baby."

"I can't. Where would I go? My mother's? She sold me! And I think Ms. Kat might have had something to do with me getting kidnapped."

"What? Why'd you say that?" Quianna responded, "There's a lot I have to tell you, another time. Have you seen my mother?"

"No, actually, I haven't but the police have been here looking for her."

"The police? Oh wow!" A knock came on the door. "Mr. Boots, let me call you back." She approached the door slowly to look through the peep hole, fearing it might be Toddy or the police. But it was just room service with the breakfast Mrs. Lee had sent up for her.

Kat's Change of Heart

Kat was getting ready to leave the hospital with Mr. Morales in their luxury vehicle and blurted out, "I can't do this no more Bizzi, I've been in this drug game too long. I'm hurting people and those babies mostly. I watched those kids grow up and I hurt them, or at least I had a part in it, not that I wanted that. When I saw Nia in that truck, I was gonna go after her, but I lost them in traffic. The truck turned the corner and I lost them! I was going against everything you needed me to do. I don't want this life anymore! We have to stop this mess! I want out! You live in Puerto Rico, I live here, and we never see each other!" Kat burst into tears.

"What...are you talking crazy woman! We make a lot of money!" He laughed nervously as his accent grew thicker. Kat really knew how to get to Bizzi's soft spot, but she was asking him to give up his empire, which he built from the ground up. It was the only thing that made him king on the island.

Kat pleaded, "Babe, look at me. I can't see out of my eye and the doctor says it may be permanent! I just want you to take me to our home in Puerto Rico and live a normal life. I just want to relax. I will call Jean, get her to come over to your hotel and stay with me tomorrow. Oh yeah, you never met her." Bizzi interrupted, "Actually, I have. She helped me try to find you. Then I sent my guys over to your building and they got locked up trying to get into your apartment. Someone called the police." Kat reiterated her point, "See? They love me and I betrayed them! Oh my God. What have I done?" Then Kat looked up and said, "I love Jean, she's a great friend, so loyal. How'd you like her?"

Puzzled, Bizzi asked, "What do you mean?"

"Well, she was cool wasn't she? She's helpful like that!"

Bizzy dismissed her remark, "Let's get you to the hotel." Kat continued, "She's my best friend. She got my back. Not only do I trust her with business, but I trust her with my life! She was the only one who knew about you. I used to talk about you to her all the time. We'll get to spend some time together this week." "Enough!! Enough talk about her! I want to take care of you!" Kat looked at him crazy, "What the hell is wrong with you?" The nurse arrived at her room to wheel her downstairs and help her get in the car. Kat's left eye was covered with a bandage, but with her right eye, she observed Mr. Morales' face and knew something wasn't right.

They proceeded to the car and Kat was all in her feelings. Thoughts ran through her mind, she knew her husband hadn't always been faithful. He often used his power and arrogance to draw the attention of thirsty women. Kat knew Jean wasn't one of those women, but he was manipulative and calculating.

"Babe, are you hungry?" Kat stayed quiet, staring straight ahead at the raindrops on the windshield. The driver then looked through the rearview mirror, "Mrs. Morales, Mr. Morales asked if you'd like something to eat?" Kat snapped out of it and turned her head quickly, which caused a lot of pain. "Shut your got damned mouth! I don't need you to tell me what he said! I can hear!" "Hey! Hey! Que pasa? What is this you refer to me as 'He'? What the hell is wrong with you woman?! You respect me!"

"Respect you?! Ha! How can I? There's nothing to respect! First of all, you kill people with guns and drugs, and you sell little kids to grown men. Second, you're a cheater Eric Morales with a dumb ass nickname like Bizzi...why 'cause you get busy with the women? But you really have the smallest junk I ever seen in my life! Trust me...your swag and money is all they're after. Ha! Respect? Matter fact, take me to my house! I don't want to go to your hotel. Take me home now! Now!"

Morales was humiliated by her defiant tongue and became furious. "You are going with me! I'm not letting you out of my sight again!" Kat directed the driver again, "Take me home! If you want to come home with me, Bizzi, you can. but I'm not going to New York!" He replied, "No. You will go where I tell you to go!"

"No the hell I won't, and you're not the boss of me! I've been putting up with your shit for years. And never said nothin' but I don't like the lifestyle you live! We're separated, and I know you cheat on me and that you're living with someone in

Puerto Rico. I'm done!" He grabbed her arm forcefully, "Who the hell do you think you are? You'll listen to me and that's that!"

"I'm not your damn servant, you damn punk! You got people surrounding you to protect you because you can throw your money around, but you can't fight your way out of a paper bag! I'm not scared of you! And this all started because I asked you about my friend Jean. You tried it, didn't you? You tried to screw her, but she turned you down didn't she? You, dumbass!"

"Actually, no she didn't. She was easy and she's not your friend. Yes, I had her, and I'll have her again if I want to!" Kat burst into tears and told the driver, "Let me out!" Seeing that he had hurt her, Morales instructed the driver, "Take her to her house." He tried to console her, but Kat threw his hands off her, "Keep your disgusting hands off me! Don't ever touch me and I mean it!" They began to tussle in the back of the Black Yukon Denali. In that moment, it didn't matter that she was his sweetheart, he smacked the shit out of her. Kat was crushed and memories of her past with Black Bear came back, Morales had never treated her like that. She gave him a repugnant look, "I'm done. I want a divorce!" Turning towards the driver once more and grabbing his collar, she said, "Let me out of this truck now!" Morales added,

"Let her ass out! She wants out so bad, let her!" The truck pulled to the side on Rt. 22 in Newark. As she opened the door, she reached back at Mr. Morales and scratched him in his eyes.

Eric hollered in pain and held his face. He grabbed her dreads with his left hand and banged her face against the head rest. Her nose started bleeding, she was in no shape to be in a domestic scuffle coming home from a critical head injury. "You dumb bitch! You can really get out now." Kat slid out in front of a furniture store on Rt. 22. She yelled back, "You'll get yours!"

"Are you threatening me?!" as he checked his face for blood. Through the open door, Kat looked him dead in his eyes and said, "Yes, it's a promise!"

"I'll take care of you, just like I took care of your friend Jean and she better deliver what I told her to deliver or her ass is mine again!"

He reached over to her side, slammed the door and they sped off. Kat was left standing on the side of the highway with a head injury and bloody nose. No phone, no money and only one good eye. She started to cry, upset about the way he treated her and the lack of empathy he had for her. She was mortified that he would hurt and take advantage of her friend after she helped him.

The light rain turned heavier, so she tried walking faster, eventually seeking shelter from the rain. She went into the furniture store to ask if she could use their phone. The cashier looked at her wounds, "Ma'am? Are you okay? Your nose is bleeding." Kat answered, "I'm fine. My car broke down and I slipped in the rain. Listen, I need to make a call. Can I please use your phone?" "Yes, sure." He picked up the receiver and handed it to her. Kat called Jean's apartment not knowing she was no longer there.

After several rings, she got voicemail, so she left a message. *"Jean, this is Kat. I don't know what's going on. I was in the hospital. Larry beat me up, Shae's boyfriend. I'm not sure, but I think my husband might have hurt or threatened you. I apologize for whatever that bastard did to you. I will call you later tonight. Please answer. I want to get his ass. He put his hands on me. Please answer when I call back. This isn't my phone so don't call this number back but answer the phone later at 10, love you girl."* Then, she called Shae to come and get her. Shae answered, "Sure. Give me the address, I'll be right there. We were worried about you!" Kat cried, "Please hurry!" They hung up and Kat waited in the store.

Chapter 24

Larry and Rico in Atlanta

On their journey to Atlanta, Rico talked to the girls as they shared stories of how their pimp treated them, how he ultimately got killed, and their lives after his death as 'renegades' which is what they were called. Shawna told Rico she was beaten repeatedly by Marty, her pimp. "He didn't like me much and was hard on me. I hated him. I was glad they blew his ass away." Larry asked, "Who killed him?" "Don't know and don't care. I'm just glad his ass is gone."

Marva laughed, "You know what happened to him! She had a jawn who was in love with her ass. Well, he watched Marty hit her one too many times and shot his ass up!" Larry jumped back in, "Seriously? You told him to do that?" Shawna smirked, "No I didn't! Marty used to put me in the trunk of his car for hours if I didn't make his money every night. If I screamed while I was in there, he'd beat me with a plastic bat he called 'Wilson'. After he beat me, he'd make me kiss 'Wilson' goodnight. Sick piece of...."

Jacqui interrupted, "Yeah he'd make me stay up if I didn't make my quota. If I fell asleep, he'd beat me with 'Wilson', then send me back out to work. I would be so glad to get a customer. I would fall asleep while they did their thing. One time the dude left without paying. I got beat with 'Wilson', and thrown in the trunk. I fell asleep in there. Boy was it hot." They laughed as she continued, "He threw a dirty ass cat in there with me one time. I was scared. That cat was buggin' and he won too. I swear I passed out three times. I was so scratched up he couldn't send me out for a week. He never did that shit again." "His ass went too far. I remember that night I put sugar in his tank," Shawna laughed and so did the others.

After a few seconds of silence, Rico said, "Well, listen, I need ya'll to recruit for us. One hundred dollars for a run-away, and another $100 if it's a boy. Nobody over seventeen or younger than twelve. They're easy to train. I don't want them to look me in my face, they have to keep their head down when they are in my presence. They'll call me and Larry, daddy. They better not look another pimp in the eyes because they'll take them from me. Then I'll have to pay to get them back. You will be my "bottom," Lee Lee. I'll pay you for keeping house. You can take care of us. If you get someone not following the rules you bring them to me, and I'll take care of it or Larry will. Shawna, you'll be in charge of getting all the girls to the doctors and shopping for them. After we get established, we'll get a house for all of us, but right now we'll be in the hotel. Larry, you'll wine and dine and spoil the hell out of these girls. Make them feel like no one else in the world loves them but you. I'll take on my girls and you do yours. Marva, you'll handle the boys.

Jacqui inquired, "What's my part? I want to get paid!" Rico continued, "You can pull the girls from the club." Shawna asked, "Are we getting paid over our normal money?"

"Look!" Rico aggressively replied, "You're getting a place to sleep, clothes, nails, and hair done, medical treatment and money in your pocket or for food. If you recruit you get a hundred dollars." Marva yelled out, "Oh snap! I'm 'bout to be paid!" Shawna blurted out, "I don't know if I want to get these kids in this game." Rico tried to convince her, "Just think of it like this, they already out there all you're doing is helping them along and you'll be getting paid in the process. Shit they were the ones who ran away anyhow!" Lee Lee interrupted, "So... we don't have to trick?" Larry interjected, "Hell yeah you do! We're gonna make this money, get a house, a big house...then ya'll can stop tricking."

When they reached Atlanta, they got three rooms at a hotel. Larry and Rico stayed in one room; Shawna and Lee Lee shared another; and Marva and Jacqui were in the last one. Larry went to the other two rooms after everyone got settled to tell them they were having a meeting in his room. The girls left for the meeting. Rico started the meeting with specific orders, "We'll use your rooms for your clients and showers between clients. We're going shopping now, so you can get your personal items. We'll go over prices and all the money comes back to us. I'll collect the money at the end of the day. If you have any problems, Larry here has hands of steel. Just call. We're going to get phones. Let's be clear, they're not your phones. They belong to the house. Don't fuck up! Let's make this money! I'm making a page for us when we get back from shopping. We'll do some other sites. I'll go to the strip clubs and work on getting ya'll in there."

Lee Lee yelled, "I'm excited!" And, just as she started saying something else, she started coughing uncontrollably. Larry asked, "Ay, you alright? You look under the weather."

Lee Lee cleared her throat and answered, "Yeah I'm good, I think my tea went down the wrong way." The meeting was over, and everyone headed back to their rooms to get ready for their shopping trip. Lee Lee was the last one to get up. Larry asked again, "Are you sure you're okay? You don't look good at all!"

"I think I'm going to lay down for a little."

Rico agreed, "Okay. We'll go shopping and come back." When they did, pictures were taken in their outfits. Then, they retreated to their rooms. Thirty minutes passed and Rico called the rooms. "Let's go, we got work! Get dressed, we're going to the strip club. We got two hours before ya'll hit the stage." Everyone got up and started getting ready except Lee Lee. Larry checked on their progress and saw Lee Lee hadn't moved since she left the meeting. "Yo dude! Get up, let's make this money!" Lee Lee grabbed her head, "I can't. I'm not feeling too good. Ya'll go ahead." Larry persisted, "Get up! We're all going!"

"No…I'm not goin!"

"Yes the hell you are! We're going to make this money tonight!"

"Man go ahead I said I'm not going! I don't feel good! I'll catch you on the next one!"

Larry grabbed the bed sheets from under Lee Lee and flipped her straight on the floor right up against the dresser. "Now I'm not gonna say it again. Get your shit on now!"

Lee Lee with barely any strength said, "Are you fucking crazy! You better be glad I'm sick!"

"Oh yeah!" Larry started beating the mess out of Lee Lee. She was so weak she could only lay there and take it, hollering and moaning with every blow and kick. Shawna screamed for him to stop, using her body to block the punches. Marva ran to the room and tried grabbing Larry's shoulders to pull him back while Jacqui went for his arms. They saw how helpless Lee Lee was in her state, not even trying to defend herself. Larry grabbed Jacqui and threw her into the mirror. Then he took Marva by the arm and flipped her over his shoulder without even turning around, tossing her right on top of poor Lee Lee.

Larry addressed them all as he caught his breath, "Now let's get this shit straight, get your asses in the car, don't try me again!" Jacqui struggled to get up while pulling glass out of her butt. Lee Lee had a hickey on her head and was bleeding from her nose. Marva tried to gather herself to help Lee Lee. Then Larry stomped to his room and told Rico what had just went down, bragging about how he got those lot lizards straight.

Rico's eyes widened, "What the hell is wrong with you?" Suddenly he started crying and Larry looked confused, "Yo, you crying over those lot lizards?"

"No, man. I just found out they buried my uncle!" Rico left his room to check on Lee Lee and finds them in terrible condition. "Damn ya'll can't go to the club tonight looking like that. What happened?" "His crazy ass got mad because Lee Lee said he was too sick to go with us," Marva answered. "So he pulled him out of the bed and beat his ass. We tried to protect Lee Lee but he threw us around like rag dolls."

Lee Lee laid motionless on the side of the bed with her knees on the floor bleeding on the checkered comforter. Rico tells them, "I'll cancel the strip club for tonight. Get some rest and we'll resume tomorrow. Listen, Larry ain't no joke! That was light what he did to you. Don't let him get mad, it's not nice at all." He shook his head and returned to his room.

Mr. Tony's Burial

The coroner had determined that Mr. Tony died about 20 minutes before his store was to close. The security tapes and the ongoing investigation hadn't brought Mr. Tony's case any closer to getting solved. No one saw anything that could help the detectives. Meanwhile, everyone prepared for his burial.

Mr. Tony's body was laid out so nicely in his coffin. He had been dressed in his dark brown suit with a crimson red tie and brown shoes. People from all over the city poured in to pay their last respects and say their final goodbyes. Reverend Briggs was asked to do the eulogy. Mr. Tony's family had flown in from Puerto Rico. Quinn also flew in from Los Angeles but couldn't go to his uncle's funeral or wake because he'd blow his cover as a family member. Quinn hadn't even let Eric Morales know that the last girl they had was also missing from the Vintner Estate. He knew somehow Morales would find out and come after him. It wasn't safe for Quinn to be out. Flowers were lined at each end of the casket, and the people took their seats as service started in Rev. Briggs' church. The line of people went from the front of the church to clear around the corner. His family, the church congregants, even Mr. Willie's wife showed up. The church choir sang *Amazing Grace* while drug addicts staggered in to pay their respects as well. Mr. Tony took good care of a lot of them, letting them sleep in the shed when it was cold, rainy, or if they just had nowhere to go. He'd let them stay a night or two, always treating them with kindness.

Folks kept looking at the door to see if Rico was going to walk in for the funeral. Mr. Tony's sister was there, which was just what Eric Morales was betting on. It was brilliant to get his family all there and he knew, then, Rico would get the message. Quinn wasn't able to get in touch with Rico's mom to keep her safe, but his plan was to kill Eric Morales himself for killing his uncle. But he had to be careful about Morales catching him, he planned on saying he was looking for Rico and left Quianna with the Vintner. Though Quinn still wasn't sure if the police had Quianna.

Mr. Tony had touched so many lives there was too much to tell at the funeral, so they opened up the mic for people to share their stories at the wake. Story after story showed how this man made a difference. One lady from the neighborhood said her husband left her and she had run out of food. Mr. Tony brought the food that was left over from the hot trays at the store every night for a week. He gave her money to pay her electric bill and put gas in her car. She had four children under the age of ten. There wasn't a dry eye in the room.

Quinn sat in his rented truck waiting to see any of his cousins so he could let them know they were after his aunt, but none had stepped out. Out of nowhere, a black Denali pulls up. Three men get out, one opened the back door, and it was Eric Morales himself. 'What in the hell is he doing here?' Quinn questioned, about to lose his mind.

He was boiling inside. Thoughts of Eric Morales shooting up the place and taking out his entire family ran through his head. For a second he thought Morales was there to accompany his wife, but realized she wasn't with him. Fear for his family crept back in his mind.

Rev Briggs and Sheeka

Rev. Briggs saw Sheeka for the first time at Mr. Tony's funeral. Everyone was so excited to see her like she was some celebrity. They expected the old Sheeka back, but she was so ignorant to everyone, with a stank attitude. Rev. Briggs tried to save her from this awkward moment and hugged Sheeka then began to pray over her, thanking God for her return. Some people stayed while he was praying, others left because of her demeanor. Then there were a few that just stared whispering to each other. He asked her to come with him to his office and they sat down at his desk. Rev. Briggs looked at her, "I prayed for you every day you know. That God would bring you home and He did! What did they do to you sweetheart? Let me ask you this, what can I do for you? I can't take away the pain that you've already endured but I can show you how you can get through this from here on out. I can show you how to give your pain to Jesus!"

Sheeka started sobbing, "It's all my fault. I talked them into going with Rico and those guys. I wanted to go with them! Now everything is messed up. I ruined everyone's life. I deserve to be like this!"

Rev. Briggs saw the guilt spewing from her face, "Wait, wait just a minute now!" His voice getting deeper as he spoke, "This is not your fault. In any way! You didn't make those girls go. You also didn't have anything to do with the horrible plans of those men! That's what the enemy wants you to think. He wants you to put guilt on yourself so you can't go forward and move on with your life, fulfill your purpose! What if I put something together about sex trafficking? You can be the head of it. Maybe it will be therapy for you once you talk about it. We can bring awareness to prevent others from going through your experience."

"Mmm...I don't know if I wanna live all that again."

Rev. Briggs told her to think about it and excused himself briefly to show his face at the repass, which would soon be over. He gave his condolences to Mr. Tony's family once more and then he was praying for Rico. They thanked him for sending Tony off well. Rev. Briggs thanked the kitchen staff and ushers and walked back to his office just as Sheeka was walking out. She told Rev. Briggs, "You took too long. I got to be somewhere."

"Oh, well, I'm sorry. I had to say goodbye to Mr. Tony's family. But I want you to think about speaking to the youth. You could save someone from going through the same thing. You could save a life."

"We'll see."

"Hey, Sheeka, how's your mother doing? I didn't see her at the funeral."

"Um she's fine." She hurried across the street, asking if anyone had seen Ronnie. Monster came out of the house after changing his clothes from the funeral. "Hey Sheeka!" He ran over to hug her and felt something bulky in her waistband. This was his first time seeing her since she'd been missing. "I'm so glad you're okay. I've been praying for you!" Sheeka, sounding uninterested, replied, "Yeah, yeah. I've been praying for me too. You seen Ronnie?"

Monster was concerned, "Listen, I'm so sorry you had to go through that. Do you know if Nia is okay? They still haven't found Quianna. Did they treat ya'll bad? What happened?"

"Yo, you seen Ronnie or not?"

"No, I haven't. What you need to see him for?"

"What about Ms. Kat?"

"Uh uh. She's been gone for a minute. What you up to Sheeka?" She started walking away without answering him when a vanilla envelope falls on the ground. The envelope was labeled *Shamma Temple Outreach Fund*. Monster screamed, "What the hell Sheeka?! You stole from the church? What's wrong with you?"

"Mind your damn business!" In their scuffle over the envelope, it ripped, and the money fell all over the ground. They both just stood there frozen. Monster bent down to pick it up and Sheeka grabbed a hand full and ran off. Monster collected the rest in utter disappointment and took it back to the church. He walked back to Rev. Briggs' office. Rev. Briggs saw the look on his face and said, "Hey son what's up?" Monster informed him, "I brought this back. Sheeka took it from the church. We fought over it, and this is all I could get back. She grabbed some and ran off. Do you want me to get the rest from her?" Rev. Briggs huffed, "No son, you've done enough. Good job. Thank you." Rev. Briggs looked down at the ripped envelope concerned about Sheeka's condition.

Chapter 25

Stuck in Long Beach

Quianna sat on the edge of the hotel room's bed, staring out the large window, trying to figure out what to do. Where would she go from here? She was too scared to hit the streets not knowing if Toddy would try to take her out again. Her only option was to move at night. She took her phone and called Boots again, but this time Boots texted back. *Can't talk. I'm at a wake. Call you when I get out of here, whoever this is.* Quianna looked at her phone in frustration, so she went to the sauna to try to ease her mind.

Three days had passed now, and she had to check out. She was still scared as hell of Toddy and debated whether she should call Ronnie to tell him about his brother. What would she even say? She felt totally responsible for his death because the only reason he came out to California was to rescue her. The phone rang and it was Ronnie. She sat for a moment silently contemplating if she should answer or not. With dried tears on her face, she took a deep breath and she answered softly, "Hello?"

Ronnie was excited to hear her voice, "Yo! Key, what's up baby? Man! So glad to her your voice! You good?" Out of nowhere, she blurted out, "They killed him! They killed him!" Ronnie was confused, "Say what now?" Quianna repeated, "They killed him! He's dead! I'm so sorry!"

"Wait. Slow down, Key. Who's dead? Let me talk to Ricky so he can tell me what's going on."

"Ricky is dead! He was hit by a car, a speeding car! We were crossing the street…and, and it just came at us! He pushed me out of the way and they killed him!"

"What? My brother is dead? My brother is dead!" Ronnie started crying in disbelief. Quianna's cries got louder, "Yes! I'm sorry. I'm so sorry! It's my fault. He came out here to help me and they killed him."

"Who is 'they' Key? Who killed him?" His sadness immediately turned to anger.

"Toddy, this guy from Santa Monica…his name is Toddy. He ran us down. Oh God, Ronnie, I'm sorry!" There was dead silence on the line. Quianna was still crying as she held the phone to her face waiting for Ronnie to respond, "Hello?"

"I'm here," he sounded emotionally drained, tears running down his face. He tried clearing his throat,

"Where are you? Oh my God, yo...my brother!" He turned to the side, bent down and threw up on the sidewalk, sick to his stomach at the news of Ricky's death.

Quianna replied, "Are you okay? Um, well, I have to get out of my hotel room. I don't know where I'm going from here. I'm so lost. Why is this happening to me? This is all my fault! My life is going to hell Ronnie! It's going to hell!"

Ronnie got himself together and whispered under his breath, "Damn...can't get paid now." Quianna was unsure of his words, "What did you just say?" But he didn't answer. "Answer me, what did you say?" Ronnie ended the call. Looking perplexed, she put her phone down, walked to Ricky's bag and checked Ricky's clothes; checking every pocket, then his suitcase. She found six one hundred-dollar bills in a pair of jeans. She took the money and threw the jeans on the bed. 'What did he mean now he's not gonna get paid, paid for what?' she asked herself. Then her thoughts took her to a dark place, 'I can't take this shit no more. I should just end everything! Why am I even alive?' She contemplated taking her life but always remembered Rev. Briggs telling them in Vacation Bible School that their lives weren't theirs to take, and anyone who killed themselves would go to hell. He would tell them even in dark times, there was always hope.

Hiding in Pennsauken

Te'nah had sent Monster the money she promised him. Although she went against her mother's wishes, she felt led to help Monster, never considering the risk. Te'nah sat at the dining room table and looked at her mom who was in the kitchen making lunch, "So mom, tell me this, when Ms. Kat married that man she knew he was a Sex Trafficker?" Jean nervously answered, "No, he told her maybe a year after they got married. She knew he was King Pin in Puetro Rico though."

"You know everything mom! You do know they call you nosy!" They laughed and Jean joked, "They used to call me Lois Lane!"

"Lois Lane? Who's that?"

"Ugh never mind!" Te'nah continued, "So let me get the lowdown on everybody!" Jean replied, "Okay well, who you want to know about first?" Te'nah said, "How about top floor down, Ms. Tootie." Jean reflected as she spoke, "When Tootie came here we never saw a boyfriend or Quianna's father, not even one family member. She was a little mysterious and went right back to work the day the kids went missing."

"Who does that? Some grieving mother, huh?"

Jean continued, "Now Shae always had a man. I watched her leave one and three days later she had a new one not any better than the last. She was desperate for love. She's done some real crazy stuff to keep a man. Then there's Ms. Vivian huh! A functional drunk…you seen her beat that man's ass that time?"

"Yeah, I remember. But Ms. Renee is definitely different." Jean finished, "Renee is a good mother, hard worker, a very nice lady. If I wanted anyone to make it out the 'Bricks', it would have been her. She's gonna do big things, she's got goals and she's knocking them down one by one. You know Renee made manager in a year?" Jean walked to the table to sit next to Te'nah.

Te'nah took a bite of her sandwich and continued the conversation, "So what about Mr. Boots?" Jean answered, "Boots…that's a whole 'nother story. His ass was a stockbroker on Wall Street in New York City, he was big time. He was married and lived in an upscale area in the city. They had one daughter." Te'nah interrupted, "Wait, so what made him end up living in the alley in Newark?" Jean came right out with it, "COCAINE! He was from Newark before moving to New York. But he lost everything over drugs, his family, his job and his self-esteem. Girl, he used to be fine! He had this bad Gold Cadillac…he was sleeping in it for a year probably 'til it got towed then he went to the alley."

"Wow! For real mom?" Jean added, "He still is nice looking." Then Erykah Badu's song *Next Lifetime* came on and Jean grooved to the music as she tried to clear her mind. A few more songs played on the radio. Te'nah, still not satisfied with the information she received, asked "Okay mom, what about Mr. Tony?" Jean reminisced, "Tony. He was always the same, the way you see him is the way he always was. Friendly, generous just an uplifter."

"How come you don't want to give Mr. Rex a chance?" Jean looked her daughter square in the eye, "He's country, he's from down south, you know…old fashioned, just old acting but I know he really likes me."

Te'nah wondered about her mom's feelings but changed the subject, "Well why did Mr. Willie's wife leave him?" "Oh…she was a gambler, he kicked her out. She spent all their money, they almost lost the cleaners twice."

"Wow I remember her when I was small." Jean continued to eat, "Yes, and Rev. Briggs never married. I guess he was married to ministry, he is a faithful man of God from childhood. He's always loved God."

Te'nah had so many questions for her mom, but she decided to enjoy the time with her as they sat together eating and listening to the music that played throughout their great aunt's house in Pennsauken.

Te'nah's Fate in Jeopardy

At the 'Bricks', Monster went to the mailbox on the lower level of the building by the front entrance. Two men walked up the brownstone steps and Monster opened the door for them and greeted them while he retrieved his mail.

One of the men asked, "Why do they call you Monster?"

Monster was taken aback, "Excuse me? How do you know my name?" The other man spoke up, "Why don't you answer the question?"

"I don't have to answer. I don't even know you, who are you guys anyhow?"

One of the men pushed Monster into the mailbox with his forearm to his neck. "Where's Te'nah?" Monster tried to fight back. "I don't know and if I did I wouldn't tell you anyhow!" The second man punched him in the stomach, and he buckled to his knees, the wind knocked out of him.

"We're going to ask you once more. Where's Te'nah?" The mail Monster had in his hand fell to the floor and the first man reached down, seeing Te'nah's name on an envelope. He looked at Monster, then at the other man and smiled. The envelope had her return address on the front, he smacked the letter across the palm of his hand and nodded for them to leave. The man holding Monster let him go but not without kicking him to the ground. They walked out, leaving Monster sick to his stomach and scared for Te'nah. Until then, Eric Morales' men were in big trouble. They couldn't produce anything he had asked, but this was their chance to get in right with the boss as they drove south on the New Jersey turnpike.

Though everything had gone smoothly for the initial building renovation, things inside were not so smooth for everyone. Tootie was on the run, Renee and Nia had moved out, and Jean was gone. Everyone had left the 'Bricks' except Vivian and her family. Kat moved back in and things were about to change, business wasn't going to be the same as usual. Kat called Ronnie and Ricky for a meeting and found out through Ronnie that Ricky was dead. She offered to pay for his funeral, in that moment she didn't have the heart to tell Ronnie that the drug business he'd been running was over. But Kat wanted to change her life for the better. Her grandmother always prayed she would, and the prayers were beginning to work!

Ronnie filled Kat in on everything that happened while she was gone. Patting himself on the back about how he held it down while she was missing in action. He asked, "So where were you, on vacation? I mean, you could have given me a heads up! I know you just wanted to see if me and my brother could run the business by ourselves…you know, in case one day you wanted to retire." Kat stared at him and he continued, "Even though Ricky left to find Quianna."

"Quianna?"

"Yeah. He got a call from her and Sosa was paying me big money to bring her back. I didn't tell him about it. Ricky went to get her, his dumb ass was so in love, but got killed in the process. Stupid." Tears started building up in his eyes. "I'm still going to find her though. I have to get her, that bitch got my brother killed!" Kat sat quietly contemplating the mess she had created.

Chapter 26

The Twists in Life

At the Residence Inn, Quianna gathered her stuff and headed to the lobby. She looked over at the front desk hoping she wouldn't see Mrs. Lee, so she wouldn't have to say goodbye since she was leaving so abruptly. Her taxi arrived to take her to a more affordable hotel in Long Beach. She arrived at the Montero Motel, not exactly the upscale high-rise hotel with the beach views and infinity pool, but it was nice and what she could get at sixty-three dollars a night. She flirted with the guy behind the counter and told him about her dilemma, so he got her a small discount on a room. She thanked him with a wink, though Ricky was still on her mind and thoughts of the last look on his face before he died horrified her soul.

After she got settled, she began to explore the streets to familiarize herself with her new surroundings. She turned the corner and saw a lady handing out some pamphlets. As she approached, the lady locked eyes on her. The woman called out, "Hello beautiful!" Quianna hesitantly answered, "Hi."

"I'm handing this literature out to everyone in case they run into someone who might need housing. If they are in trouble."

"In trouble?"

"Yes, if they're runaways, or into prostitution and they want out. If they've been kidnapped, human trafficked, those types of situations. It's a safe house!"

"How much does it cost?"

The woman was puzzled at Quianna's question, "It's free. Why? Do you know someone who needs help?" She placed her hand on Quianna's shoulder and looked directly into her eyes with concern.

"Yeah, I might know someone. Is it a shelter?" Quianna stared at the woman's hand still on her shoulder.

"No, it's not. We offer counseling, schooling, church services, classes on etiquette, and mostly we have fun. Listen, my name is Ms. Assata. I work there and we're open twenty-four hours. So when you're ready, we're ready for you. That's our motto."

"Okay, thanks." Quianna took the pamphlet and walked off confused, not knowing if she was psychic or a prophet. She thought, 'How did she know this was for me? Maybe I can go there if I run out of money? Hmm. That will be my next option.' "Hey young lady!" The woman disrupted Quianna's thoughts.

"Huh? Yes?"

"I never got your name?"

"Oh…it's Quianna."

"That's beautiful! Here's my personal number Quianna, again, my name is Ms. Assata. Call me anytime. Oh and we have classes and breakfast, lunch, and dinner for those who sign up for our counseling sessions. Okay?"

"Oh okay. Thank you!" She stuck the lady's card in her bra and kept walking. She passed by the address on the card but there was no sign on the building. 'I guess to keep it inconspicuous,' she thought as she shrugged her shoulders and kept going. Her phone rang and it was Ronnie calling her again.

Quianna answered, "Hello?" Ronnie started questioning here, "Key, I need to know everything so we can get my brother's body back here and you too if you want to come. I need to know everything, including your location. You should really come back home! I see you got put out of the 'Bricks.'"

"Put Out?"

"Yeah your mom's stuff is outside, fiends takin' shit! You need to come."

"I don't know anything about that, but I'm in Long Beach, in Cali. The guy was from Santa Monica, I can get you to him, just keep this number on so you can reach me."

"Okay, my moms is crazy sick about Ricky!"

"How are you holding up? I just want to tell you I'm sorry he tried to come for me and lost his life. I wish...," she started crying again. Ronnie also started crying as his voice cracked. He cleared his throat, "Just get me to whoever took my brother out. I need all the info so we can put him away nice, talk to you in about an hour." Quainna agreed and ended the call. She walked to the Noodle Shop and sat at the table to get some food, when suddenly she heard a familiar engine sound with loud pipes. She looked up and saw a Black BMW roll past the restaurant. Her heart was racing, nowhere to go but only one way out, the front door! Her anxiety was out of control, and images of Ricky's body came back to her mind, when the kitchen bell snapped her out of it!

Quianna turned around with fright on her face and the lady behind the counter yelled, "Lady, your order is ready!" She got up quickly and grabbed the bag off the counter. The lady asked, "You not want your drink?" Holding the beverage up. Quianna walked slowly back to the counter and snatched it out her hand, now wanting to leave the store, uncertain of what she might encounter on the other side the door. She presses her head on the window looking up and down the street before exiting. She took a deep breath and headed north walking swiftly but inconspicuously. Ten minutes later, she made it into the motel, and let out a sigh of relief once she reached the elevator.

Quianna sat in the chocolate colored chair in the corner of her room. Fear had overtaken her and the only person she was in contact with was Ronnie so she called him hoping he could ease her mind. Ronnie answered, "I have to take my brother's number out my phone because when it rings, I think he's gonna be on the other end." Quianna sighed, "I can't say sorry enough. I..." He interjected, "Hey, we're good Key, my brother loved you! I'm going to come get you, my brother would have wanted that." He knew using her guilt about his brother would convince her to come back to Newark and he'd get paid.

"I think that guy is riding around looking for me. I saw his car, I'm scared! Hurry up and get here! What if he comes looking for me and finds me?"

"Stay in your room, Quianna, we're flying into Oklahoma we'll drive the rest of the way. We're gonna pick up some "pieces" for me and my boys, that's where my brother went wrong. He didn't have anything to protect himself. Just hold on we're coming! Tell me where Ricky is so they can get his body flown back here, text it to me along with the address of your hotel."

"Okay, sending it now." They hung up and she turned on the T.V. to calm her nerves. The news of the famous Vintner's murder investigation came on. Still no suspects but a vague lead on a scantily dressed African American woman, late teens early twenties, who was the last one at the estate. They reported that the housekeeper found the body. Quianna grabbed the remote and shut the T.V. off falling back on the bed as tears ran down the side of her face. Then, she remembered the safe house. Quianna took the card out and called Ms. Assata. "Conqueror's House, Ms. Assata speaking, can I help you?" Quianna squeamishly replied, "Umm, never mind!" "Hello, hi do you need help young lady?"

"No. Yes...No!"

Ms. Assata reassured her, "Yes, it sounds like you do, meet me at the door. You can make it, I'll help you. Just meet me at the door and let me know when you get here."

"Okay," she placed her money under the lamp on the dresser and left for the meeting. Ms. Assata was at the door waiting, and Quianna walked in. She greeted her with a warm hug. "Were you the one that called?" Quianna shook her head yes. "Well come on, I'll give you a tour of the place." As they walk through the building, she tried to get a feel for Quianna's situation. But Quianna didn't want to talk about anything and was kind of turned off by Ms. Assata's line of questioning.

"I don't think this place is for me. Can you show me the way out?"

"Hey now don't be upset. I just need to know the services you might need, Quianna." She touched her shoulder to make her feel comfortable. "It's okay, we don't have to discuss it. Come on, the session is about to start." A man started with prayer and Ms. Assata went on the stage to introduce the Founder of Organization. It was Mrs. Lee! Quianna was shocked and uneasy. She stood up to leave, but Ms. Assata came down the steps and moved quickly to get to her, "Hey, are you leaving?" Quianna was unsure of why she was there, "Sorry, this isn't for me."

Mrs. Lee took the stage and introduced herself and the program. After her introduction of the first speaker, she left the stage and walked toward Quianna and Ms. Assata. Mrs. Lee was surprised to see Quianna. She greeted her and offered an apology for their last encounter. "I know that things didn't end well when we last saw each other but I want to make it up to you if it's alright?"

"What do you have in mind?" Mrs. Lee diected Quianna to her office and Ms. Assata returned to the session. In her office, Quianna sat on the Burgundy colored loveseat. She looked over the room and saw a prayer area in her office but in front of the prayer step wasn't a picture of Jesus, there were baby footprints and hospital pictures of a newborn.

Quianna moved up to get a closer look, "What the hell is going on? Why do you have my baby pictures in your office? Are you some sort of freak stalker?" Mrs. Lee responded, "No baby, that's not you. That's my daughter who was stolen at birth, I told you about her. I've prayed for her for 18 years."

"No…I know that is me," she studied the picture. "Yeah, I'm positive that is me, that's my baby picture. You have my picture!"

Mrs. Lee came closer and looked at Quianna's face. "What did you say was your birthdate again?"

"October 10th, just a few days ago."

"And…what hospital were you born in?" Uncertain of what was happening, Quianna gulped before answering, "Long Beach Medical, why?" As tears welled up in Mrs. Lee's eyes, she asked one last question, "Do…do you…umm, do you have a birth mark?" Quianna nodded yes.

"On your left outer thigh?" Again, Quianna shook her head. "Oh my God…," Mrs. Lee's face lit up, "Do you know what this means? Quianna! It's you! You're my child!" She moved briskly across the room to hug her but Quianna pushed back, "But that can't be! I have a mother!"

"Is your mother's name Lucretia Whealer? They call her Tootie, right?" Quianna was confused and hesitated, "Yes…that's her name, but how do you know this?" Quianna still didn't believe the possibility that this woman who lived 2800 miles away could be her mother. Her thoughts escaped her, 'The mother that raised me, that I thought loved me…is a fraud and a kidnapper, a fake?!' She went into shock and collapsed on the floor.

"Quianna! Are you okay? Listen to me, I've prayed day and night for you for 18 years! And now I have my baby back. God has protected you just like I've asked Him to. You are just as beautiful as I imagined. Thank you God! Thank you!" She went to Quianna's side and said, "But I'm curious, why are you here? What happened to you?"

Quianna ignored the question and asked, "What did you name me at birth?"

"Lilly."

Quianna chuckled, "I'll stick with Quianna thanks." They both laughed as they sat on the cream-colored silk rug. Mrs. Lee suggested they return to the session. She has a guest speaker who will be talking about Sex Trafficking. They entered the auditorium and caught Ms. Assata's eye. Mrs. Lee gave her the okay to bring up the speaker. Ms. Assata introduced Det. Armstrong, "He is the Human Trafficking Task Force Coordinator. Thank you for being here Detective Armstrong, we're looking forward to your expertise."

"Hello, I'm Detective Tod Armstrong and today I want to educate you on Human Trafficking. Sex

Trafficking is a form of modern-day slavery. Adults and children are engaged in commercial sex acts against their will. Every year, millions of men, women, and children are trafficked in countries around the world including the U.S. It's estimated that human trafficking generates billions of dollars, not millions but billions. Human trafficking is a hidden crime as victims rarely come forward to seek help, look for barriers, fear of the traffickers or law enforcement. The trauma caused by traffickers can be so great that many may not identify themselves as victims. There's other forms of trafficking, like Labor Trafficking. They're sent to homes, farms, factories, door to door sales, restaurants, construction workers, landscaping, elder care, manufacturing, forestry and housekeeping. About 100,000-300,000 kids in America are at risk for sex trafficking each year. In the U.S., it occurs mostly in Texas, Florida, New York, and here in California. Human Trafficking is a massive problem. How many people here have either been trafficked, almost trafficked, or know someone that's been trafficked? Show of hands, this is a safe place." Almost everyone in the room raised their hands. Det. Armstrong sighed, "Wow! That's horrible to know that almost everyone in here has come across some sort of trafficking."

"Who's at risk?" He continued, "U.S. citizens, foreign nationals, women, men, children, and LGBTQ individuals. There's immigration status, recruitment debt, isolation, and poverty. Because you are here at this forum you're at risk. The trafficker looks for the person that appears to be disconnected from family and friends. On their own. Someone who's stopped attending school. A prostituted child is forced to serve between 1,000 to 1,500 clients per year. Many of you in here don't look over 35, you're still at risk. I want you to know that you can fight against the trafficker. Many people who are in certain situations such as economic hardship, emotional vulnerabilities, maybe psychological or physical. However, you have the power...but you must use it! First you must recognize the signs early so you don't get trafficked. The trafficker takes you through a honeymoon stage. For girls or women, when they treat you really nice and buy you things, they gain your trust. They're really good listeners and they ultimately use the information you give them against you later to coerce, intimidate, emotionally abuse, and isolate. But you can stop this thing before it starts!"

"If you're kidnapped, that's a different story but if someone meets you and seems too good to be true, it probably is! They gain your trust, they tell you that it's just you and them against the world, they will convince you that they're the only ones who care about you. Then power of control comes on. 'If you love me, you'd do this this for me.' When you refuse, the coercion and threats come. They threaten to harm your family, to expose or shame the victim. They threaten to go to the police or immigration. They'll display weapons, destroy the victim's property or their own just to show their power. They will humiliate the victim in front of others. Play mind games like making the victim feel like it's all their fault that they're in this situation. If you can see the signs, you won't fall for the con. That's why I travel around to venues like this one, to educate men and women about this heinous crime."

"So I've told you about women and children, now I will tell you about men and boys. They can also be trafficked through Labor Trafficking or Sex Trafficking. The males are perceived as gay, promiscuous, pimps, hustlers, or buyers. They're not seen as victims who need help. People think that boys are not pimped and don't need services. There's a stigma that males should be strong enough to fight off traffickers and that they can fight off traffickers. Now we all know that every man isn't strong or very physical!" The room began to giggle as he kept talking. "They fall under the same situations as women and girls. A lot of them just need someone to talk to, and the trafficker is an open ear. There are a lot of men who want a boy for sexual pleasure, and they use physical abuse as a means to control. They are either sent to work hard for long hours which is Labor Trafficking and they get small amounts of money or none at all. If they're Human Trafficked, they are expected to sleep with a certain amount of men a night and if they don't meet the quota then they are beaten or starved. It's upsetting but it's true. I have an easy number you can remember, 1-800-CALL-FBI."

Det. Armstrong requested some water, then suggested everyone take a 15-minute break. "We'll take questions and have an open discussion when we resume. Thank You." Ms. Assata told everyone that refreshments were in the recovery room and to be back in 15 minutes. Mrs. Lee and Quianna joined the group. Det. Armstrong walked over to Mrs. Lee with Quianna standing next to her, "I have some literature I think would be useful and I have some giveaways too." Mrs. Lee was pleased to hear that. The detective looked in his bag and retracted, "Oh no, I must have forgotten them! I'll call my son and have him bring the box off my desk. I must have left it in my home office."

Mrs. Lee was a little reluctant because this was a safe house where only people who were precleared were allowed, and no one else should know the whereabouts of this facility. But Det. Armstrong convinced her that his son was safe and helped him in his operation against Trafficking and Domestic Violence. Mrs. Lee was still hesitant but conceded. He called his son. Everyone was eating and discussing the information that the detective had given them. Twenty-five minutes passed, and the session hadn't started because they were waiting on the literature which was part of the next session. The doorbell rang and Mrs. Lee went to open it, Quianna stood close by. A shadow of a young man walked through the dimly lit foyer. It was Toddy!

Indicators of Human Trafficking-

Does the person appear disconnected from family, friends, community organizations, or houses of worship?

Has a child stopped attending school?

Has the person had a sudden dramatic change in behavior?

Is a juvenile engaged in commercial sex acts?

Is the person disoriented or confused, or showing signs of mental or physical abuse?

Does the person have bruises in various stages of healing?

Is the person fearful, timid, or submissive?

Does the person show signs of having been denied food, water, sleep, or medical care?

Is the person often in the company of someone who is controlling them or their situation.

Does the person appear to be coached on what to say?

Is the person living in unsuitable condition?

Does the person lack personal possessions and appear not to have a stable living situation?

Does the person have freedom of movement? Can the person freely leave where they live?

THE NATIONAL HUMAN TRAFFICKING RESOURCE CENTER (NHTRC) 1-888-373-7888 toll free

24hrs a day 7days/week

Facts on Human Trafficking-

Trafficking is the 2nd largest criminal industry in the world, after drug dealing. Human Trafficking occurs in cities, suburbs, and rural areas. Anyone can become a victim of this crime regardless of race, gender, sexual orientation, nationality, or immigration status. What is **SEX TRAFFICKING** – the action or practice of illegally transporting people from one country or area to another for the purpose of sexual exploitation. A person younger than 18 who engages in a commercial sex act IS A VICTIM OF Sex Trafficking. Globally estimated 71% of enslaved people are WOMEN and GIRLS while MEN or BOYS account for 29%. Estimates suggest that 50,000 people are trafficked into the U.S. each year most often from Mexico and Philippines. But the United States is ranked as one of the worst countries in the world for Human Trafficking. Human Trafficking is among the world's fastest growing criminal enterprises and is estimated to be a $150 Billion a year global industry.

Eight hundred thousand people are trafficked WORLDWIDE each year. Internationally, between 20 and 40 million people are in modern day slavery today. It is easy to believe that men are all at fault for trafficking, but globally 62% are men while 38% are WOMEN. Human Trafficking can happen in many situations, including COMMERICIAL SEX INDUSTRIES STREET PROSTITUTION, STRIP CLUBS, MASSAGE PARLORS, ESCORTS SERVICES, BROTHELS, and INTERNET. Other places you may see trafficking is in FACTORIES, FARMS, LANDSCAPING AND CONSTRUCTION. In 2018, over half (51.6%) of the criminal human trafficking cases active in the U.S. were cases involving CHILDREN. The U.S. Dept of Labor has identified 139 goods from 75 countries made by child labor or forced labor. You have probably handled or bought products that were made by a trafficked person. Some of the goods include coffee, computers, fireworks, furniture, cotton, clothes, gold, and footwear to name a few. Then there is Domestic Servitude, it's usually a cover for exploitation such as a live-in maid or grounds keeper.

Now let's get closer to home: NJ is RIPE FOR HUMAN TRAFFICKING! NJ is centrally located between the northern portion of the East Coast and the tri-state metropolitan region of Philadelphia, Baltimore and Washington, DC. It's easily accessible by car, bus, truck, van, train, boat and plane. NJ has the potential to be one of the country's major entry, transit, and destination states for trafficking. Who's at RISK? U.S. citizens, foreign nationals, men, women, children; youth in foster care, in the juvenile justice system, runaways, homeless, and LGBTQ individuals. Traffickers stop at nothing! They even prey on people with disabilities to gain access to their public benefits. In NEW JERSEY 83 % of victims are US CITIZENS.

How are people lured into Sex Trafficking?

The traffickers target and recruit their victims by appearing to offer help or pretending to be a friend or potential romantic partner. They weigh in on their victim's vulnerabilities; an unstable home, family dysfunction, search for a better life, lack of employment, history of physical or sexual abuse, substance abuse. Traffickers promise a good paying job, modeling careers, a loving relationship, or new and exciting opportunities. With the romance aspect, it's called the Honeymoon Stage, where they wine and dine you and offer promises that never come to pass. They gain your trust and turn you away from family and friends. They are a listening ear while gaining information about family and personal matters that you would only share with someone close, then they control the victim using the very information shared so intimately against them. Traffickers sometimes use substance dependency and addiction to keep control of the trafficked person. Some traffickers purposely supply drugs to vulnerable people to break down their resistance and coerce them into forced labor or sex. The truth is that the recruitment process usually takes place over a long period of time, it includes brainwashing and grooming tactics. Trafficking can happen anywhere, anytime, day or night. Some people are kidnapped and made to traffic immediately. They are usually transported to another state or country. This happens a lot with runaways as they are promised shelter and food to eat, but they have no idea it comes at a cost!

Traffickers gain the trust of the victim, then they are introduced to the world of trafficking by saying, "If you love me you will do it, this will help us financial." Once in the game of trafficking the tables turn, you are now made a human trafficking slave! Later they are told a quota has to be met. When a victim wants out of this lifestyle, the trafficker tells them that they owe a debt, and it must be paid before they are released to be free. The debt isn't realistic and can never be paid off. Victims are brainwashed and made to feel that only the trafficker cares for them, the manipulation and seclusion from family and friends has the victim at a disadvantage. The information that the victim has given the trafficker will be used against them. They will say, "Your mother works at such & such place" or "She lives at 123 long street. If you try to run away or call for help, I'll kill her! No one wants you, you left your family, you've been gone so long they don't even want you anymore."

The trafficker begins to groom the victim. Grooming is manipulating someone's emotions to gain control of them. Groomers use jealousy, possessiveness, insecurity, intimidation anger, and accusation.

This is the way it works: they (1) TARGET THE VICTIM-GAINING TRUST OR INFORMATION (2) FILL A NEED (3) ISOLATE THEM (4) BEGIN ABUSIVE BEHAVIOR (5) MAINTAIN CONTROL!!!

Once entered into the world of Human Trafficking, victims can become so indoctrinated that their traffickers can take them out in public and no one would ever suspect the terrible truth. The victims are beaten, starved for days, made to stay awake until the quota for that day is met. They are sometimes made to service 15 jawns a night. The victim is to turn all monies over to the trafficker. As once communicated the victim gets none of the money but will do all the work.

In a correctional facility, inmates are solicited and coerced while behind bars by other inmates who are called recruiters. These recruiters coerce female inmates into working for the traffickers. The traffickers would have the recruiters identify vulnerable inmates who will be released soon. Traffickers would converse with them via mail and promise to take care of them when they are released. The trafficker puts money on their books as an act of good faith and arrange for them to be picked up when they are released. When they walk out to what they think is freedom, the traffickers are right there to lead them into the world of slavery.

Signs of Sex Trafficking

- Lacking official identification or documentation
- Living at their place of employment, security measures that appear to keep people inside an establishment (bars covering the insides of windows)
- Not being allowed to be in public alone, avoiding eye contact, adhering to scripted or rehearsed responses in social interaction
- Checking into hotels or motels with older males referred to as boyfriend.

Exhibiting signs of abuse or neglect

- Appearing malnourished, destitute, or lacking personal possession

- Physical injuries such as burn marks, bruises, or cuts
- Tattoos or branding
- Untreated sexually transmitted diseases
- Habitually withdrawn, depressed, distracted or checked out

These are some signs if your child is still at home. Sudden or unexplained changes in behavior.

- Unexcused absences; overly tired in class
- Sexualized dress or behavior
- Older boyfriend or new friends with different lifestyle
- Wearing expensive apparel; displays of money with no clear source
- Gang

Victims can be trafficked and still go to school and live at home. Parents need to be aware of new friends, a change in the child's behavior, getting into trouble with the law. Young people are being targeted in foster homes to run away with someone who befriends them and convinces them that they can be free and lead them straight to a trafficker's hands. The trafficker gives them a place to live and a horrible life to go with it. Traffickers move the victims from state to state for several reasons. So they won't be easily found, so they can depend solely on the trafficker, so they will feel powerless. With drugs, the drugs have to be bought, packaged, and sold. But with Human Trafficking, the victim can be sold over and over and over again. The average life expectancy of a child victim is 7 years. The average victim of Human Trafficking is raped over 6000 times.

NAMES of TRAFFICKERS:

FAMILIAL TRAFFICKERS - children or minors living at home are pimped out by a family member.

ROMEO PIMP- a pimp uses grooming and manipulation to force his or her victims into sex trafficking.

GUERILLA PIMP - a pimp who uses violence, abduction, threats, or drug use to force his or her victims into sex trafficking.

GANG CONTROLLED - women and girls are forced into sex trafficking as their contribution to a gang for protection or initiation.

CATFISHING - Pretending to be someone else, a fake account on social media twitter or Instagram. Grown men messaging young girls. They manipulate girls to like them then they fall in love with them.

ORGAN TRAFFICKING

Organ harvesting has been tied to human trafficking and has become a booming business in the 21st century on a global scale. Forced organ harvesting is when people are killed for their organs. Trafficked body parts are harvested by any means necessary and are gladly received, no questions asked by the person willing to pay top dollar for a kidney, heart, liver, or corneas. At times, criminal organizations have engaged in kidnapping people, especially children and teens. Victims are killed and their organs harvested for the illegal organ trade. Kidneys are by far the most popular organ on the Black Market. The waiting times are extremely short and at times even vital organs are booked in advance. Therefore, it's not surprising that they're also one of the most expensive things to illegally purchase.

Kidneys were $400,000 in 2013, legally. There were 16,896 kidney transplants performed in the U.S., though over 100,000 people were on the waiting list. In the BLACK MARKET, they're only $200,000.

Livers are $557,000 because of a rise in liver disease from cirrhosis or hepatitis etc. which is also leading more people to require transplants. On the BLACK MARKET, the COST WAS $157,000.

Hearts obtained legally are worth $997,700 but on the Black Market, the cost was $119,000.

WE CAN HELP! KEEP YOUR EYES OPEN & SAY SOMETHING!

No matter if you are wrong, you might be just right! You can call the hotlines, someone will come out and check out the situation. They would rather you say something and be wrong, than be right and never say anything.

NJ HOTLINE- 855-363-6548

The National Human Trafficking Resource Center is a national anti-trafficking hotline and resource center serving victims and survivors for human trafficking and the anti-trafficking community in the United States. The toll-free hotline is available to answer calls from anywhere in the country, 24 hours a day, 7 days a week, every day of the year in more than 200 languages.

Victims can call the hotline at 1-888-373-7888

THE SALVATION ARMY- 267-838-5866 in Pennsylvania

Delaware has an array of services to help victims. They also have a text line- Polaris BeFree Texting: Text "BeFree" to (233733)

WHAT CAN WE DO TO HELP? BE VIGILANT! KEEP YOUR EYES POSTED!

Warning signs that an individual may be being trafficked:

Physical abuse such as burn marks, bruises, or cuts.

Unexplained absences from class

Overly tired in class

Withdrawn, depressed, distracted or checked out

Bragging about making or having lots of money

Less appropriately dressed than before or new expensive clothes, accessories, or shoes

New tattoo. Tattoos are often used by pimps as a way to brand victims. Tattoos of a name, a symbol of money, or barcode could indicate trafficking.

Older boyfriend or new friends with a different lifestyle

Talking about wild parties or inviting other students to attend parties

Showing signs of gang affiliation (colors, notebook doodles of gang symbols

NATIONAL RUNAWAY SWITCHBOARD 1-800-RUNAWAY

IF YOU NOTICE A GROWN MAN WITH YOUNG GIRLS AND MAYBE THE GIRLS ARE DRESSING A LITTLE PROVOCATIVE, IT MIGHT BE HUMAN TRAFFICKING. PLEASE CALL THE HOTLINE! MANY TIMES, IF YOU APPROACH THE VICTIM THEY WILL DENY BEING TRAFFICKED EITHER DUE TO FEAR OF THE TRAFFICKER OR BRAINWASHING. CALL THE AUTHORITIES. LET THEM DO THEIR JOB. MAYBE JOT DOWN A LICENSE PLATES MAKE OF CAR, DESCRIPTION OF PIMP AND VICTIMS, DESCRIPTION OF VICTIM AND CLOTHES.

If you work in these Industries, please take notice:

Healthcare, Hotel and Motels, Home Health Aides, Police officers, Firemen, for trafficking signs. If a pimp is present, he or she will probably do all the talking for them and answer for them. Try to separate the victim from the trafficker and ask questions and call authorities. All of these occupations can potentially run across sex trafficking or human trafficking.

Look also at Nail Salons, Hair Braiding Shops or Truck Stops. Farm laborers and landscapers. If you notice that the person sleeps where they work, it's also a red flag! Family members trafficking family members.

Thank you for your time and willingness to help save our children!

Made in USA - Kendallville, IN
1218488_9780578815732
12.29.2020 0833